TEEN TITANS GO!

STONE ARCH BOOKS
a capstone imprint

STONE ARCH BOOKS™
Published in 2014
A Capstone Imprint
1710 Roe Crest Drive
North Mankato, MN 56003
www.capstonepub.com

DC Comics
1700 Broadway, New York, NY 10019
A Warner Bros. Entertainment Company

Cataloging-in-Publication Data is available at the Library of Congress website:
ISBN: 978-1-4342-9216-2 (library binding)

Summary: Starfire and Beast Boy are wild about their new clothes from designer D.D. Ammo, but they seem to be having a hypnotic effect on everyone who wears them. This can only mean one thing: Mad Mod has come to Jump City! Will Starfire and Beast Boy be Mad Mod's fashion police, or will the villain stay a cut above the rest?

STONE ARCH BOOKS
Ashley C. Andersen Zantop *Publisher*
Michael Dahl *Editorial Director*
Sean Tulien *Editor*
Heather Kindseth *Creative Director*
Alison Thiele *Designer*
Tori Abraham *Production Specialist*

DC COMICS
Tom Palmer Jr. Original U.S. Editor

Printed in China.
032014 008085LEOF14

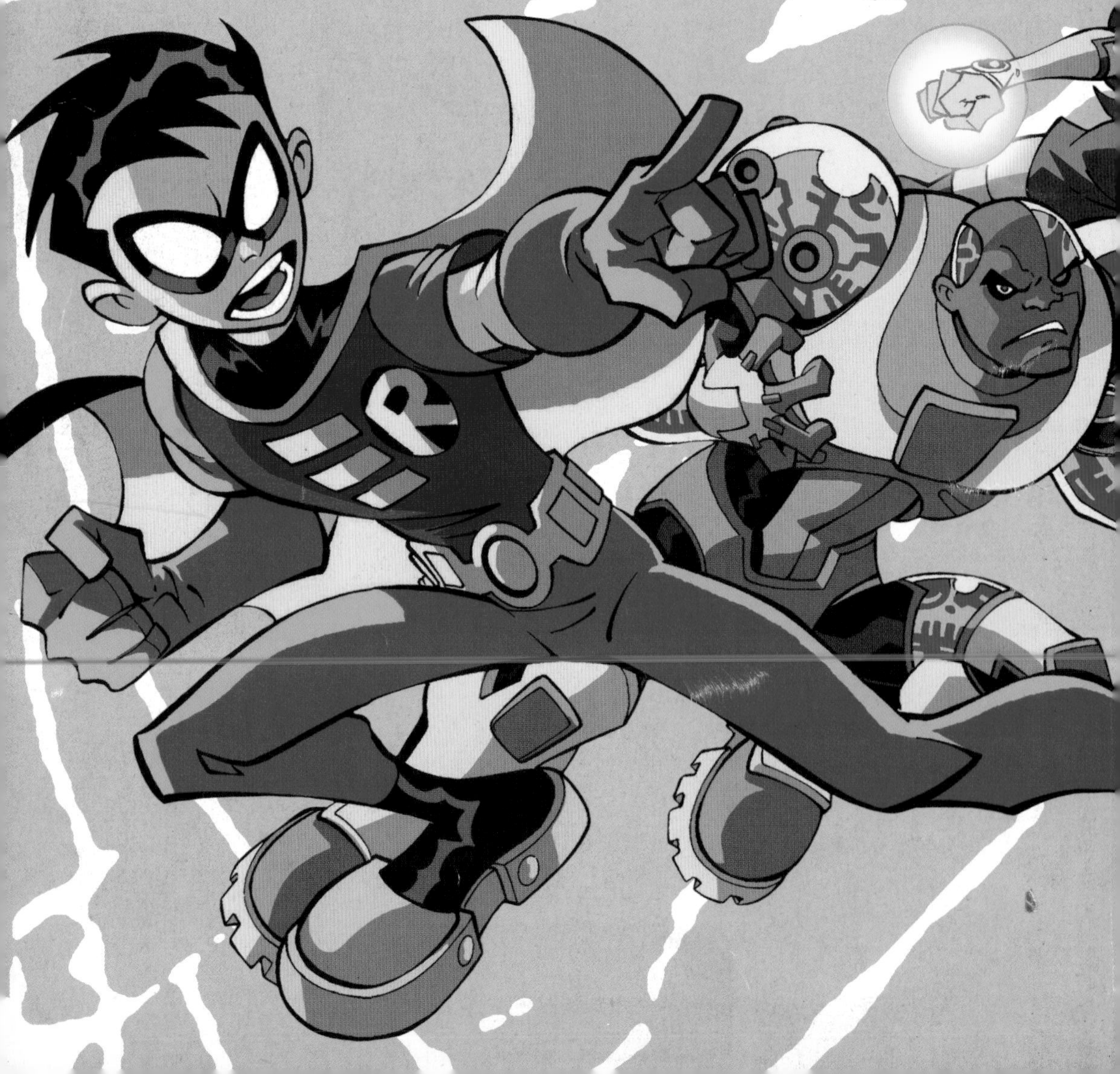

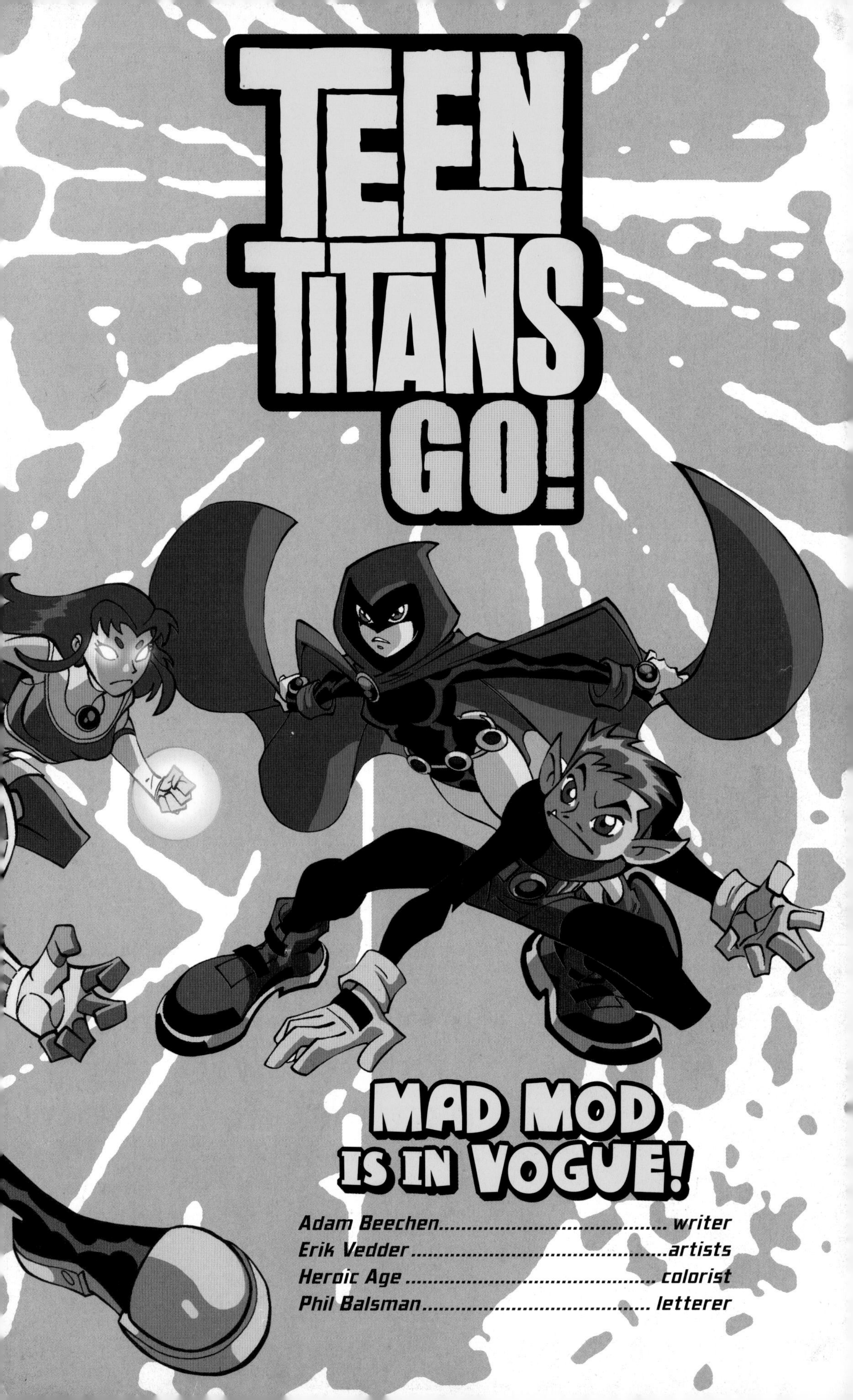

TEEN TITANS GO!

MAD MOD IS IN VOGUE!

Adam Beechen... writer
Erik Vedder ....artists
Heroic Age .... colorist
Phil Balsman... letterer

TEEN TITANS GO!

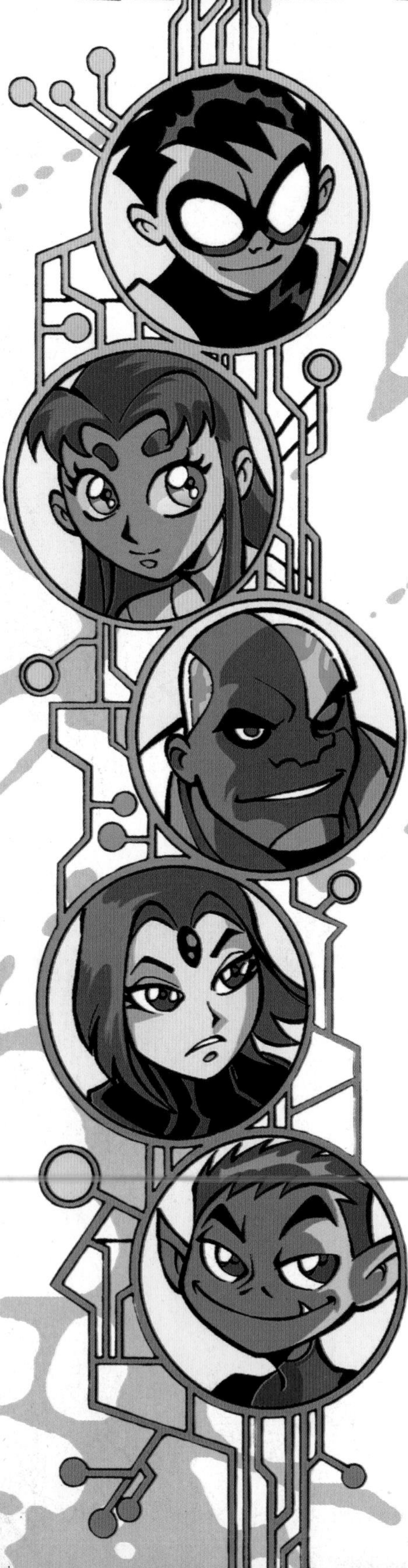

ROBIN

REAL NAME: Dick Grayson

BIO: The perfectionist leader of the group has one main complaint about his teammates: the other Titans just won't do what he says. As the partner of Batman, Robin is a talented acrobat, martial artist, and hacker.

STARFIRE

REAL NAME: Princess Koriand'r

BIO: Formerly a warrior Princess of the now-destroyed planet Tamaran, Starfire found a new home on Earth, and a new family in the Teen Titans.

CYBORG

REAL NAME: Victor Stone

BIO: Cyborg is a laid-back half teen, half robot who's more interested in eating pizza and playing video games than fighting crime.

RAVEN

REAL NAME: Raven

BIO: Raven is an Azarathian empath who can teleport and control her "soul-self," which can fight physically as well as act as Raven's eyes and ears away from her body.

BEAST BOY

REAL NAME: Garfield Logan

BIO: Beast Boy is Cyborg's best bud. He's a slightly dim but lovable loafer who can transform into all sorts of animals [when he's not too busy eating burritos and watching TV]. He's also a vegetarian.

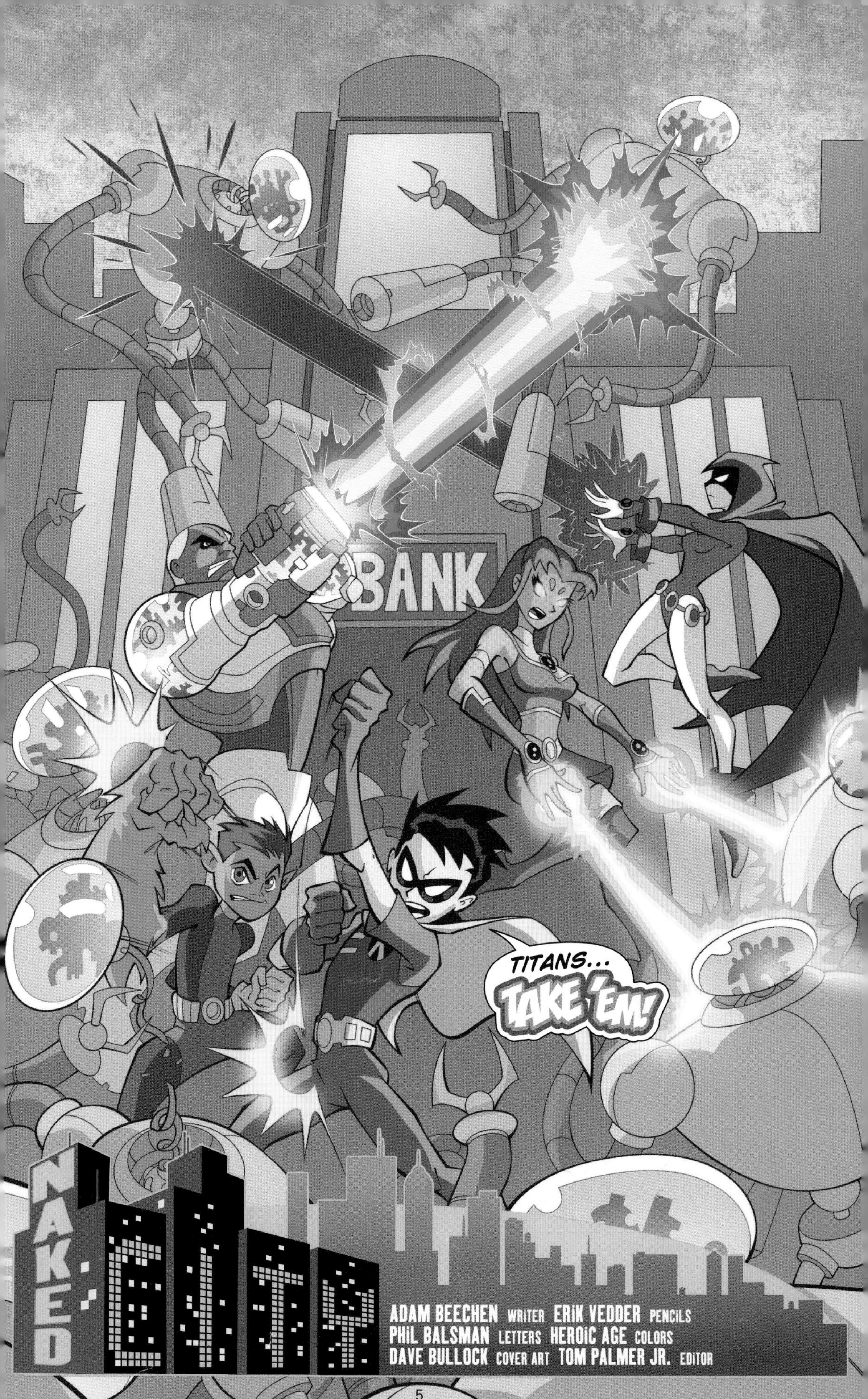
BANK
TITANS... TAKE 'EM!
NAKED CITY
ADAM BEECHEN WRITER ERIK VEDDER PENCILS
PHIL BALSMAN LETTERS HEROIC AGE COLORS
DAVE BULLOCK COVER ART TOM PALMER JR. EDITOR

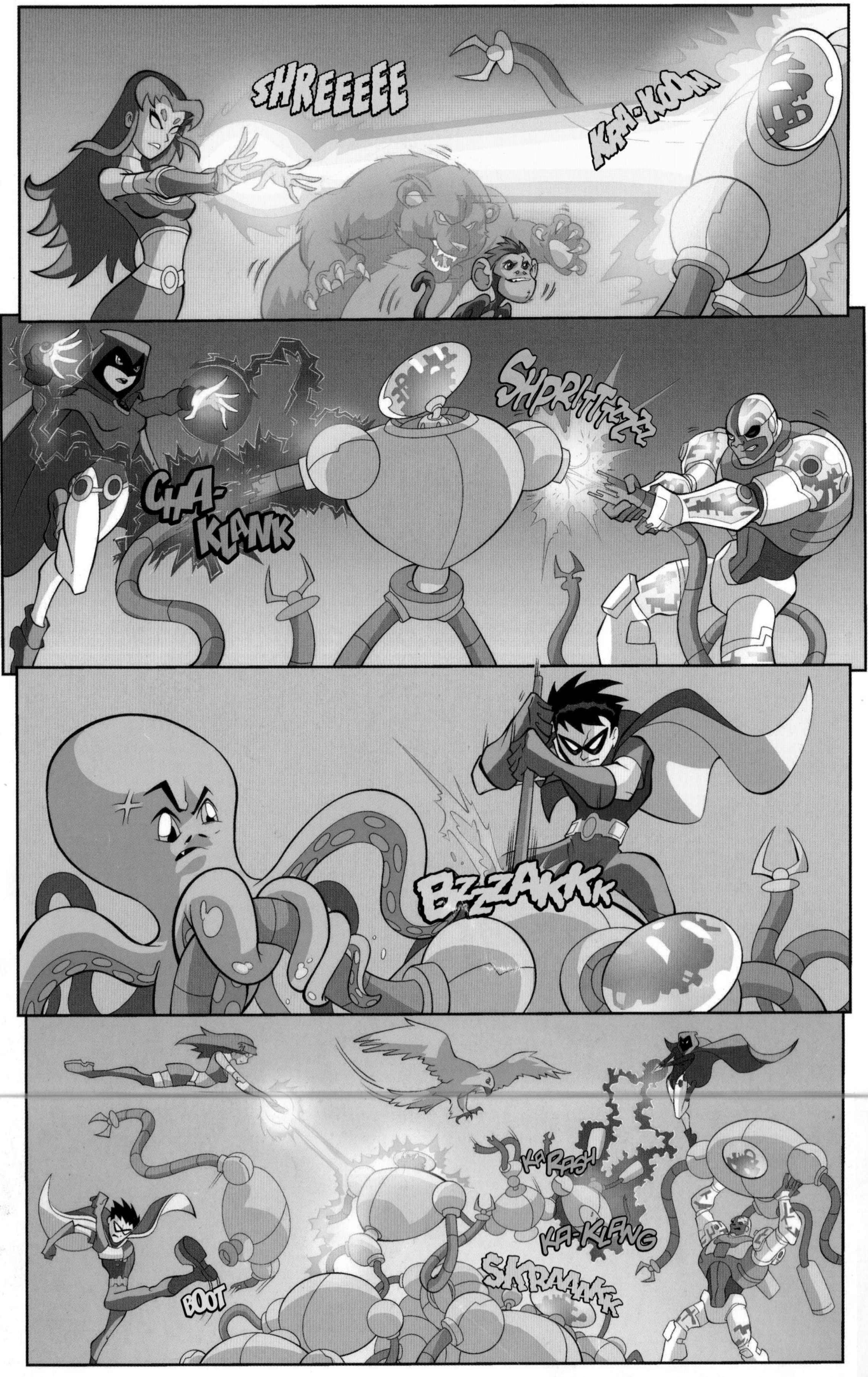
SHREEEEE
KA-KOOM
SHPRITTTZZZ
CHA-KLANK
BZZZAKKKK
KA-RASH
KA-KLANG
SKRAAAKKK
BOOT

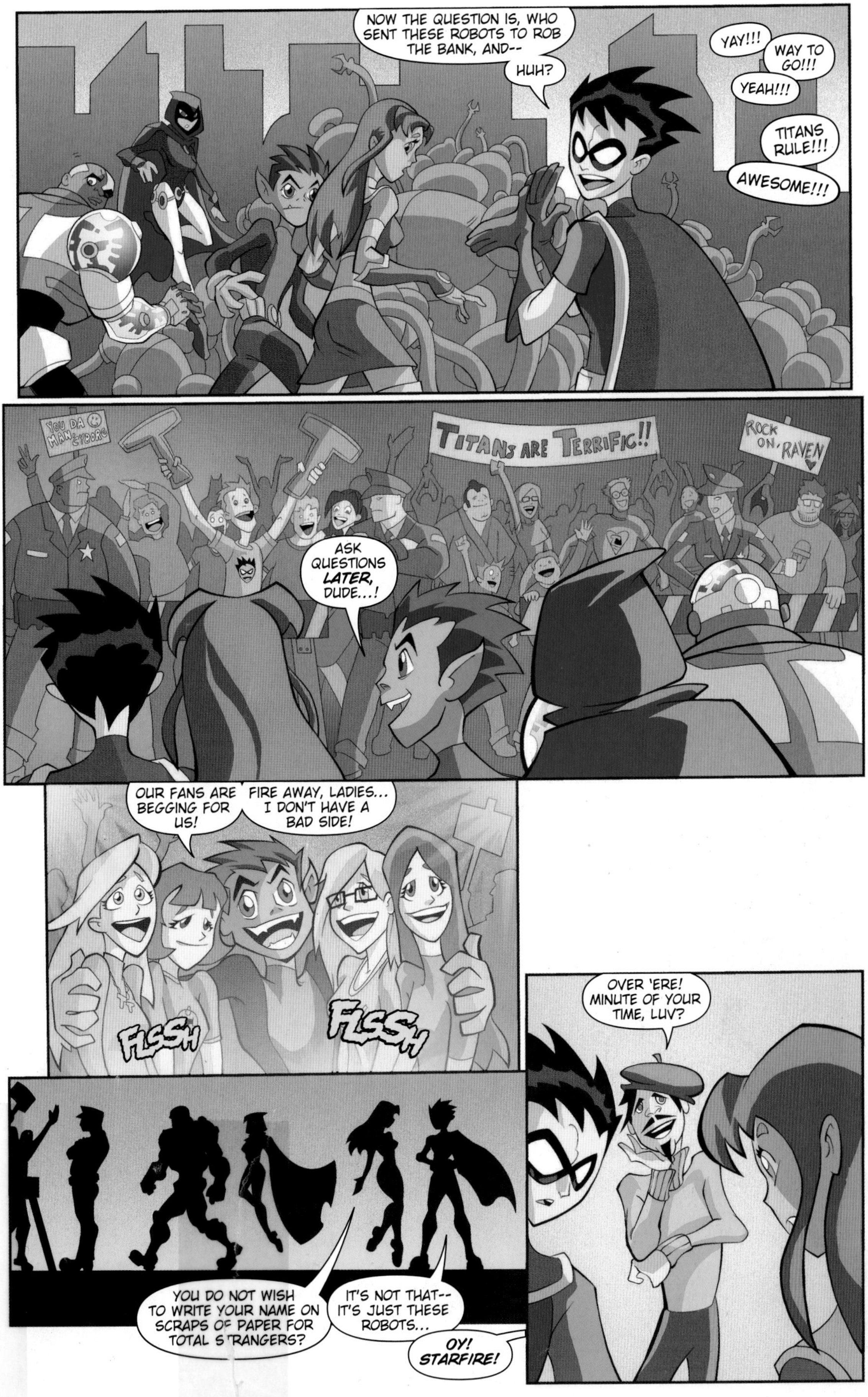
NOW THE QUESTION IS, WHO SENT THESE ROBOTS TO ROB THE BANK, AND--
HUH?
YAY!!!
WAY TO GO!!!
YEAH!!!
TITANS RULE!!!
AWESOME!!!
YOU DA MAN CYBORG
TITANS ARE TERRIFIC!!
ROCK ON, RAVEN
ASK QUESTIONS LATER, DUDE...!
OUR FANS ARE BEGGING FOR US!
FIRE AWAY, LADIES... I DON'T HAVE A BAD SIDE!
FLSSH
FLSSH
YOU DO NOT WISH TO WRITE YOUR NAME ON SCRAPS OF PAPER FOR TOTAL STRANGERS?
IT'S NOT THAT-- IT'S JUST THESE ROBOTS...
OVER 'ERE! MINUTE OF YOUR TIME, LUV?
OY! STARFIRE!

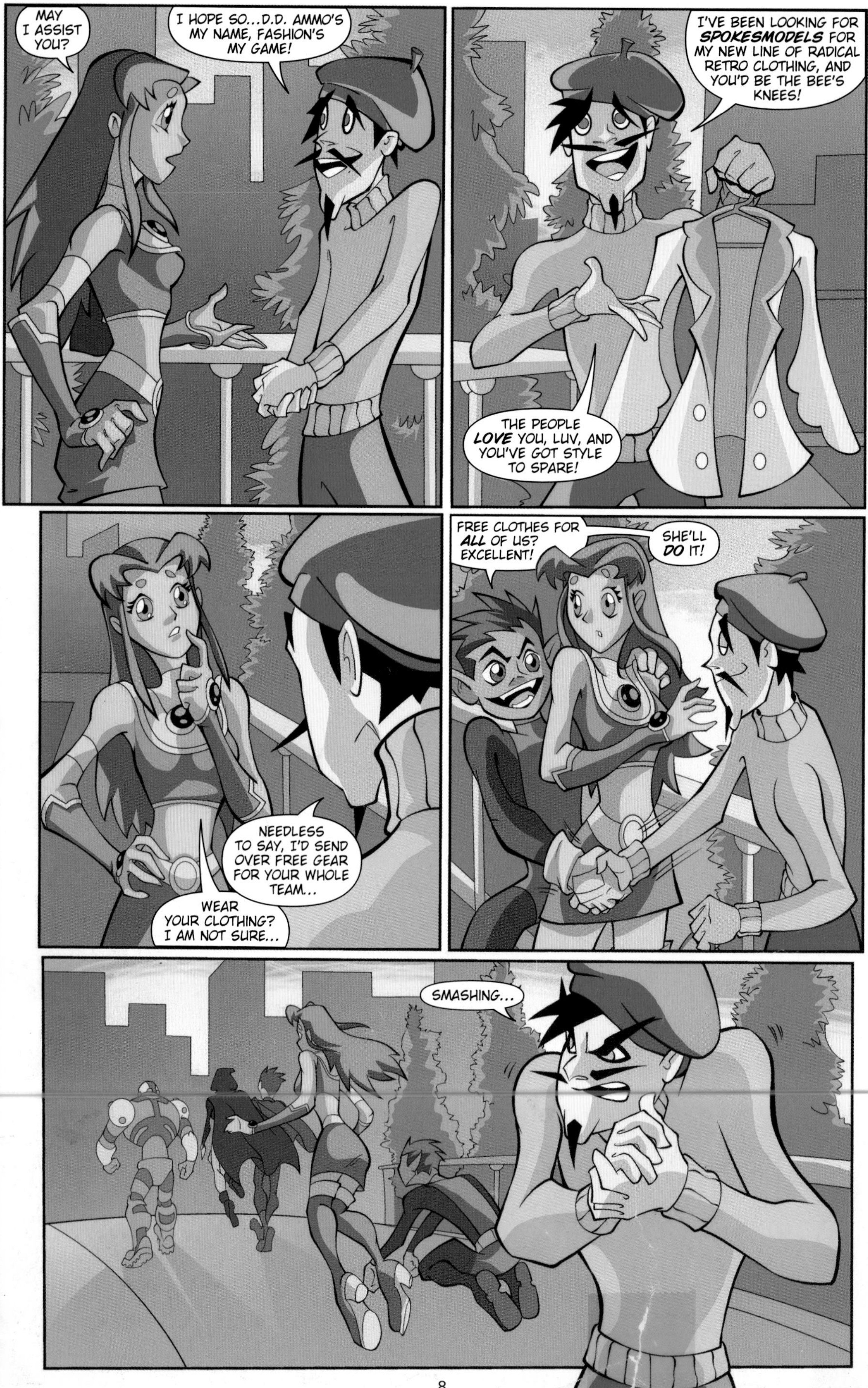
MAY I ASSIST YOU?
I HOPE SO...D.D. AMMO'S MY NAME, FASHION'S MY GAME!
I'VE BEEN LOOKING FOR SPOKESMODELS FOR MY NEW LINE OF RADICAL RETRO CLOTHING, AND YOU'D BE THE BEE'S KNEES!
THE PEOPLE LOVE YOU, LUV, AND YOU'VE GOT STYLE TO SPARE!
NEEDLESS TO SAY, I'D SEND OVER FREE GEAR FOR YOUR WHOLE TEAM...
WEAR YOUR CLOTHING? I AM NOT SURE...
FREE CLOTHES FOR ALL OF US? EXCELLENT!
SHE'LL DO IT!
SMASHING...

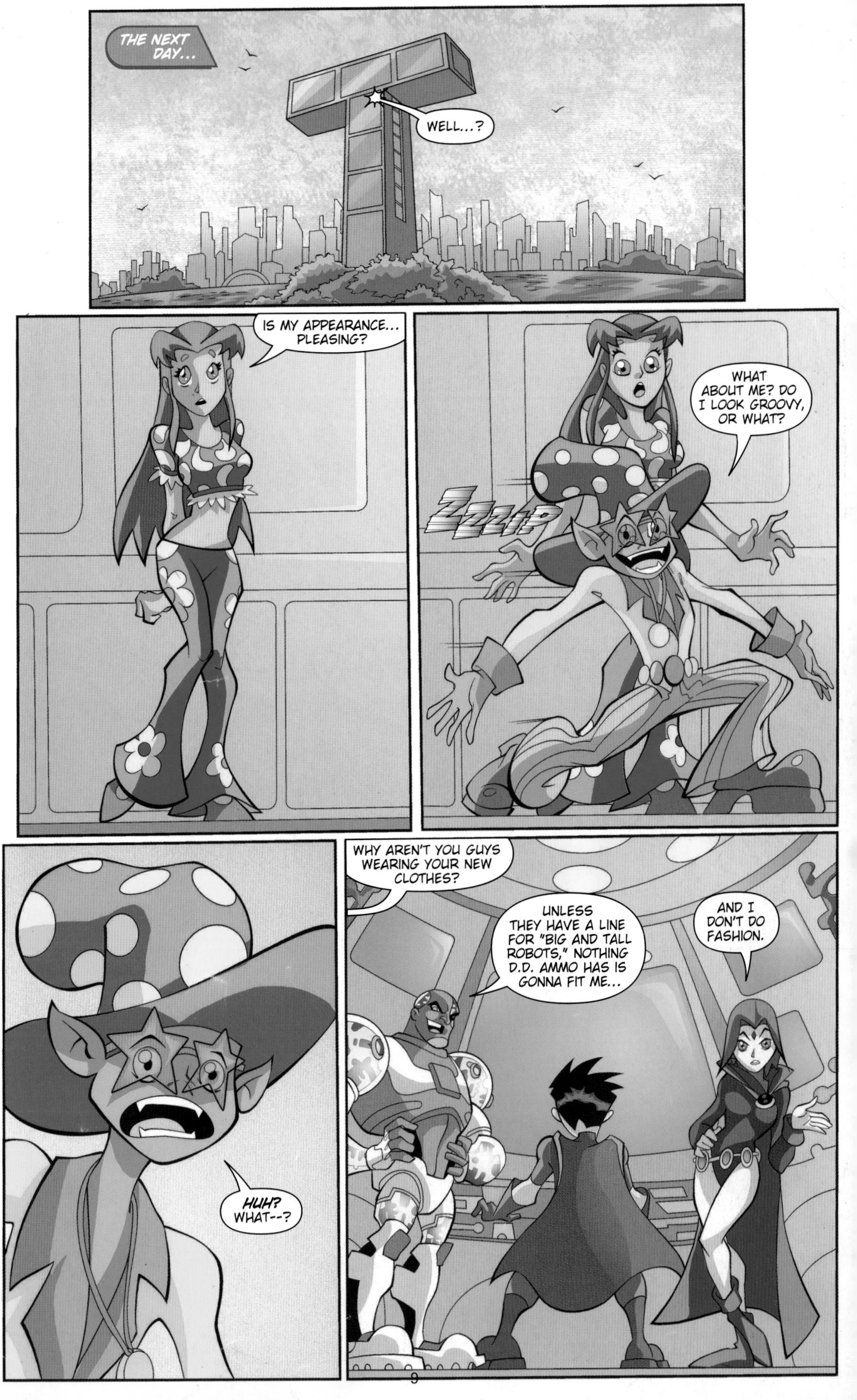
THE NEXT DAY...
WELL...?
IS MY APPEARANCE... PLEASING?
WHAT ABOUT ME? DO I LOOK GROOVY, OR WHAT?
ZZZIP
HUH? WHAT--?
WHY AREN'T YOU GUYS WEARING YOUR NEW CLOTHES?
UNLESS THEY HAVE A LINE FOR "BIG AND TALL ROBOTS," NOTHING D.D. AMMO HAS IS GONNA FIT ME...
AND I DON'T DO FASHION.

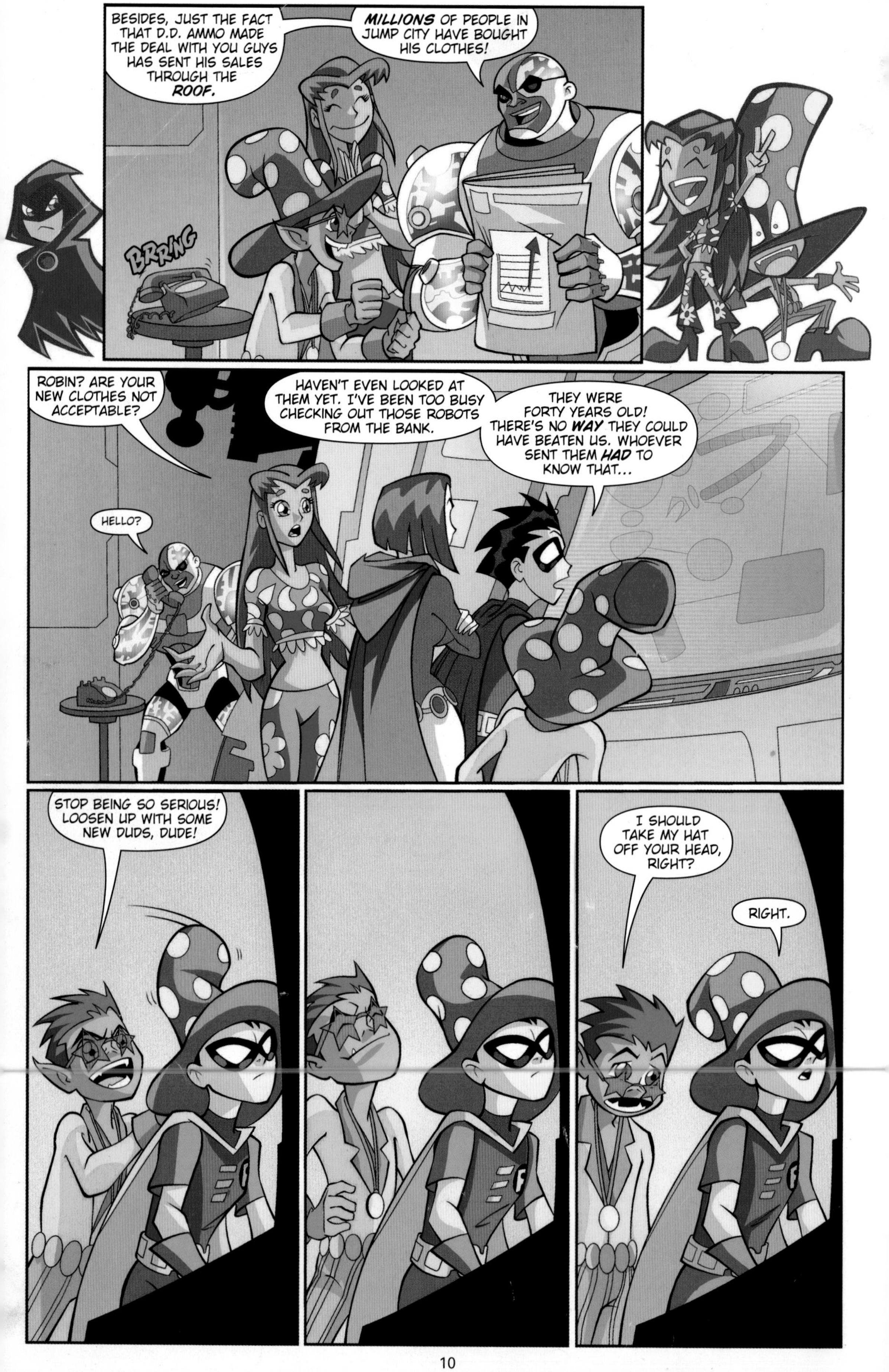
BESIDES, JUST THE FACT THAT D.D. AMMO MADE THE DEAL WITH YOU GUYS HAS SENT HIS SALES THROUGH THE ROOF.
MILLIONS OF PEOPLE IN JUMP CITY HAVE BOUGHT HIS CLOTHES!
BRRING
ROBIN? ARE YOUR NEW CLOTHES NOT ACCEPTABLE?
HAVEN'T EVEN LOOKED AT THEM YET. I'VE BEEN TOO BUSY CHECKING OUT THOSE ROBOTS FROM THE BANK.
THEY WERE FORTY YEARS OLD! THERE'S NO WAY THEY COULD HAVE BEATEN US. WHOEVER SENT THEM HAD TO KNOW THAT...
HELLO?
STOP BEING SO SERIOUS! LOOSEN UP WITH SOME NEW DUDS, DUDE!
I SHOULD TAKE MY HAT OFF YOUR HEAD, RIGHT?
RIGHT.

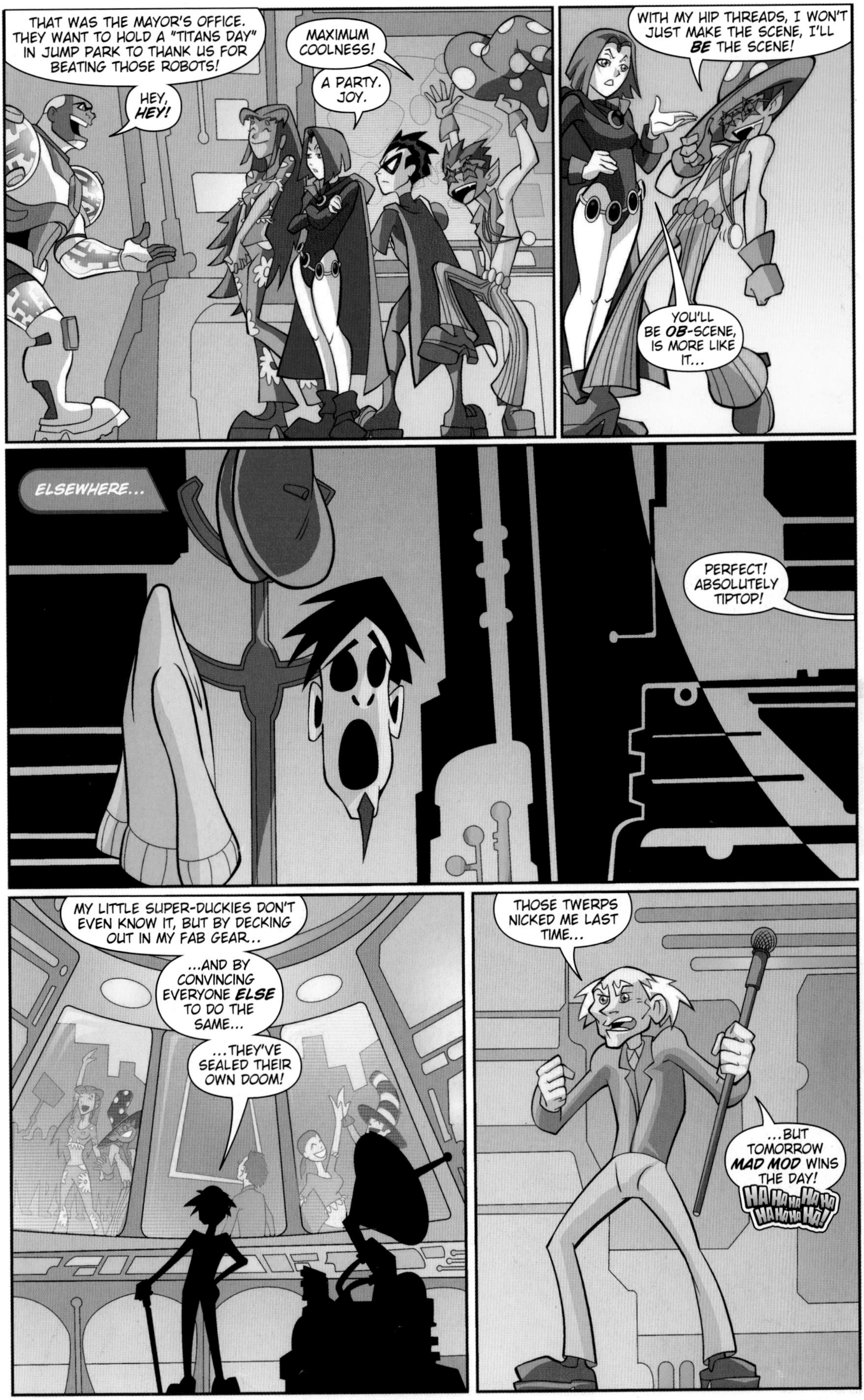
THAT WAS THE MAYOR'S OFFICE. THEY WANT TO HOLD A "TITANS DAY" IN JUMP PARK TO THANK US FOR BEATING THOSE ROBOTS!
HEY, HEY!
MAXIMUM COOLNESS!
A PARTY. JOY.
WITH MY HIP THREADS, I WON'T JUST MAKE THE SCENE, I'LL BE THE SCENE!
YOU'LL BE OB-SCENE, IS MORE LIKE IT...
ELSEWHERE...
PERFECT! ABSOLUTELY TIPTOP!
MY LITTLE SUPER-DUCKIES DON'T EVEN KNOW IT, BUT BY DECKING OUT IN MY FAB GEAR...
...AND BY CONVINCING EVERYONE ELSE TO DO THE SAME...
...THEY'VE SEALED THEIR OWN DOOM!
THOSE TWERPS NICKED ME LAST TIME...
...BUT TOMORROW MAD MOD WINS THE DAY!
HA HA HA HA HA HA HA HA HA!

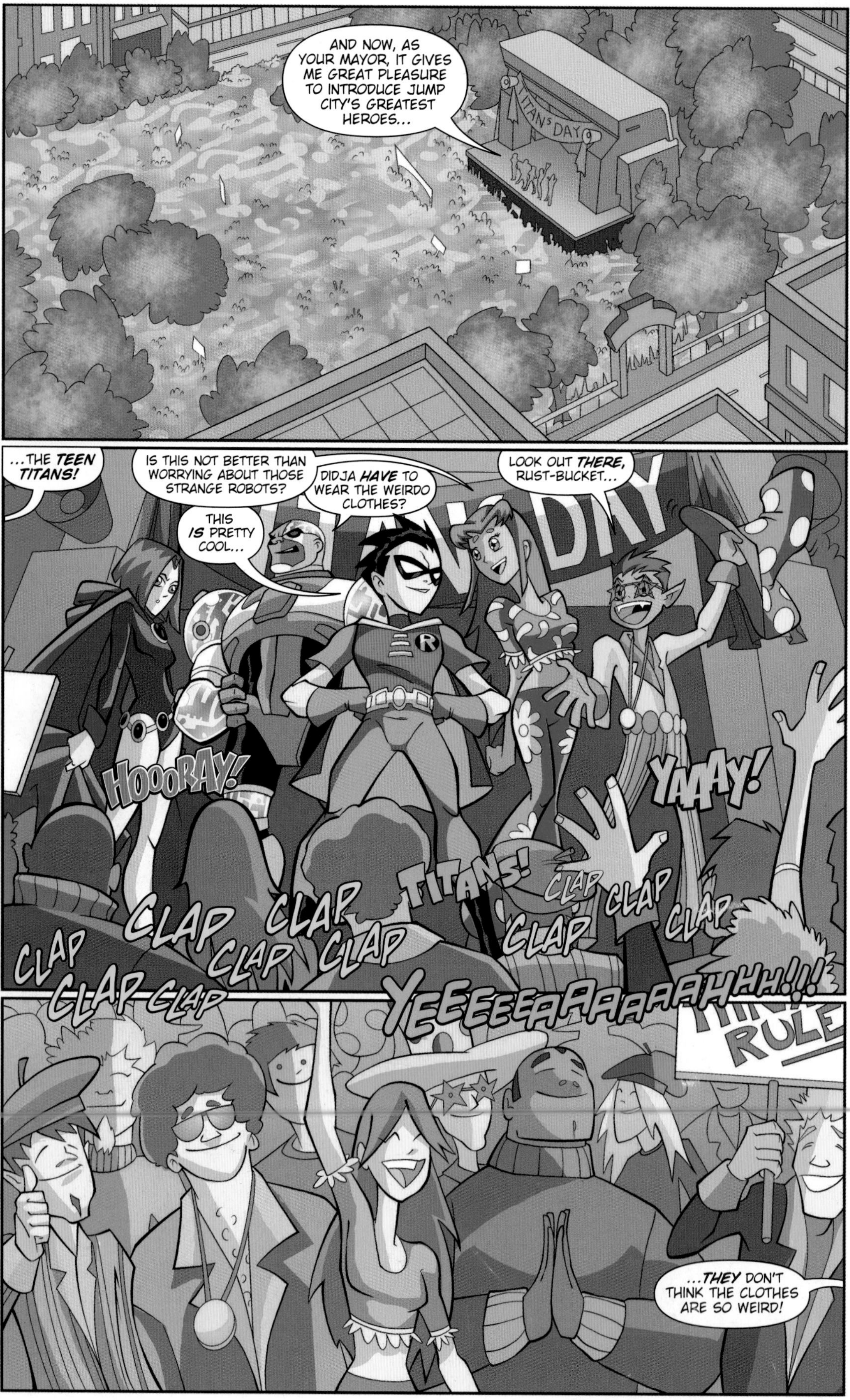
AND NOW, AS YOUR MAYOR, IT GIVES ME GREAT PLEASURE TO INTRODUCE JUMP CITY'S GREATEST HEROES...
...THE TEEN TITANS!
IS THIS NOT BETTER THAN WORRYING ABOUT THOSE STRANGE ROBOTS?
THIS IS PRETTY COOL...
DIDJA HAVE TO WEAR THE WEIRDO CLOTHES?
LOOK OUT THERE, RUST-BUCKET...
HOOORAY!
YAAAY!
TITANS!
CLAP CLAP CLAP CLAP CLAP CLAP CLAP CLAP CLAP CLAP CLAP
YEEEEEAAAAAAAHHHH!!!
RULE
...THEY DON'T THINK THE CLOTHES ARE SO WEIRD!

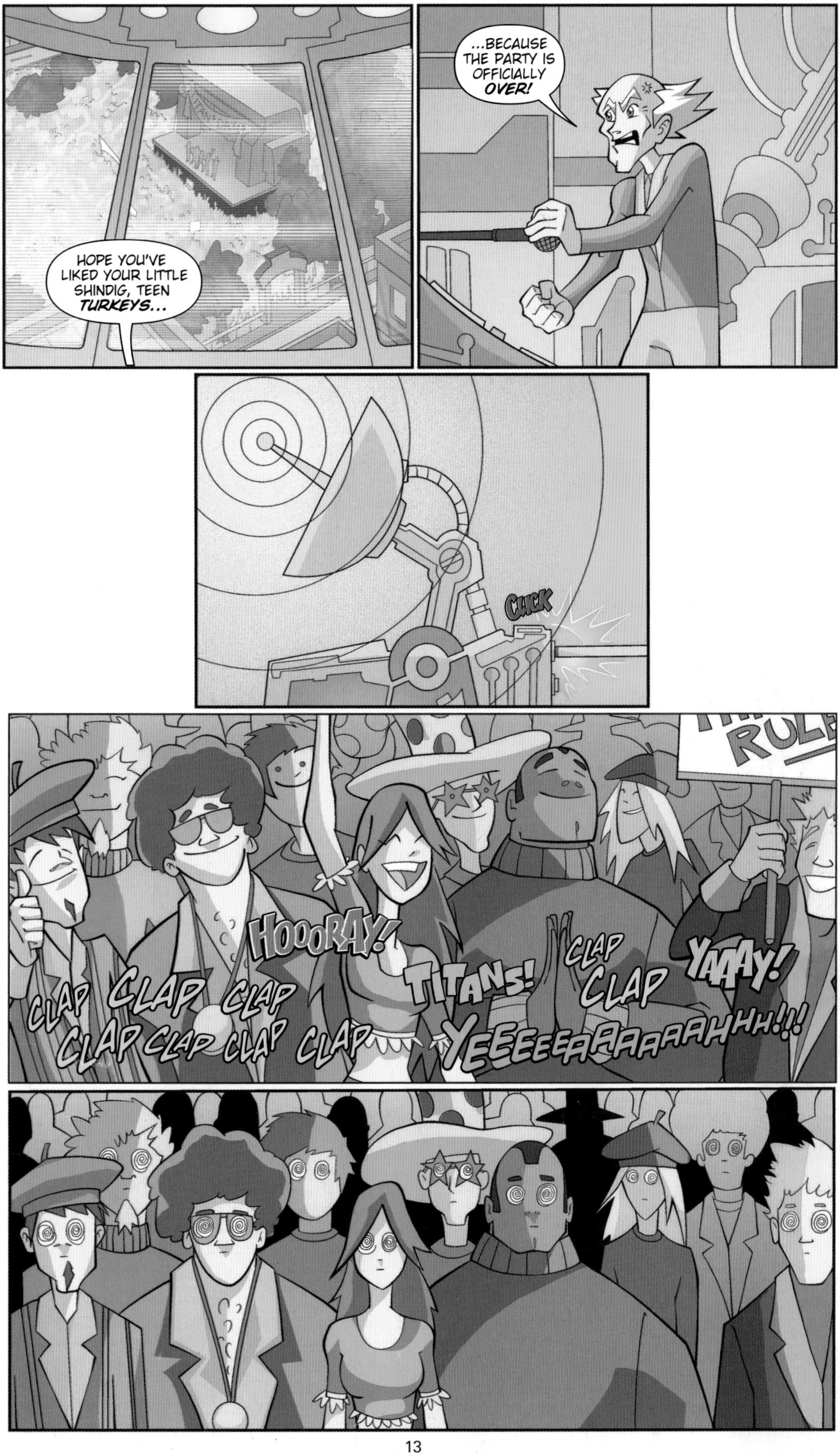
HOPE YOU'VE LIKED YOUR LITTLE SHINDIG, TEEN *TURKEYS...*
...BECAUSE THE PARTY IS OFFICIALLY *OVER!*
CLICK
HOOORAY!
TITANS!
CLAP CLAP
YAAAY!
CLAP CLAP CLAP
CLAP CLAP CLAP CLAP
YEEEEEAAAAAAAHHH!!!

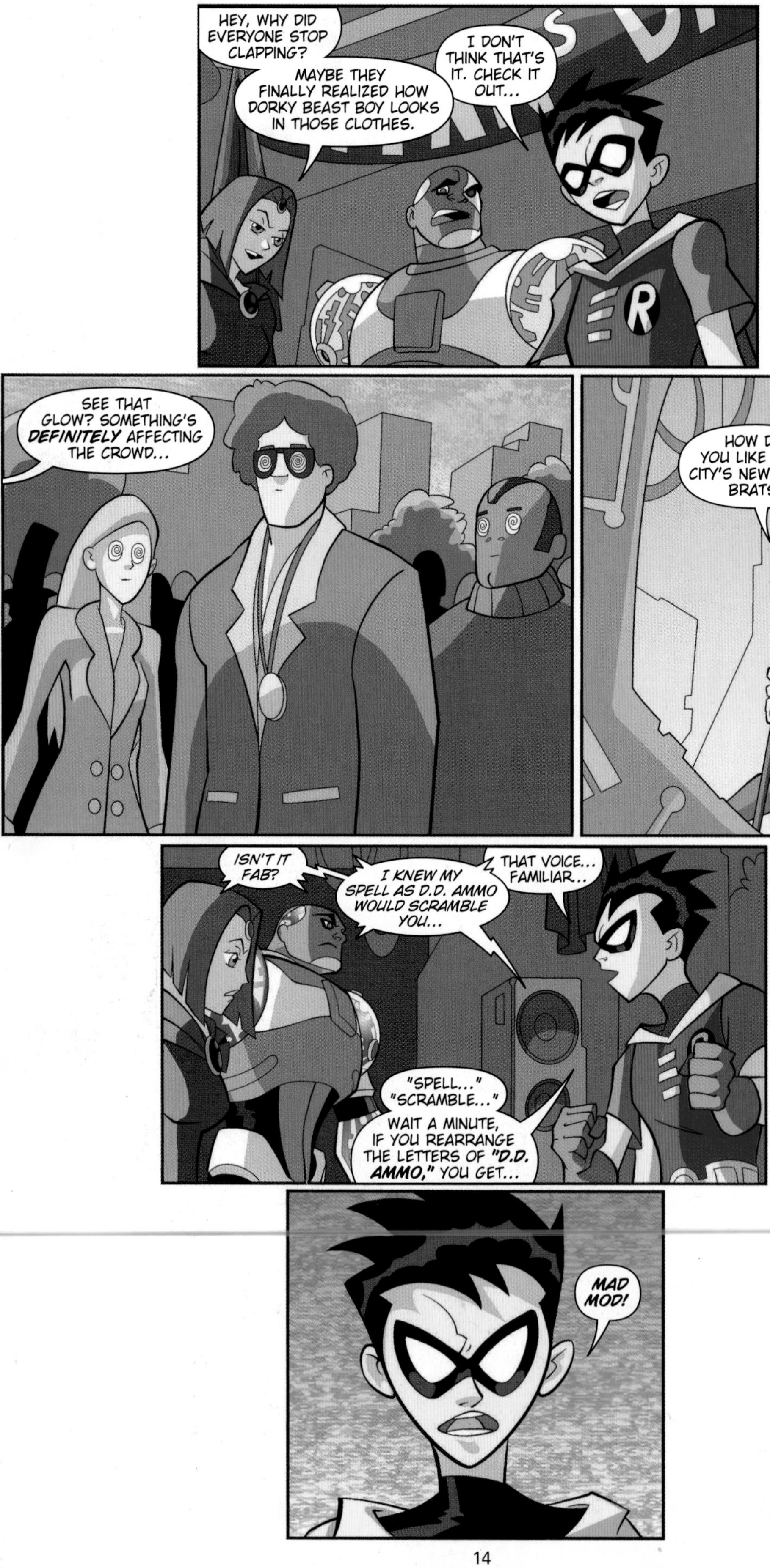
HEY, WHY DID EVERYONE STOP CLAPPING?
MAYBE THEY FINALLY REALIZED HOW DORKY BEAST BOY LOOKS IN THOSE CLOTHES.
I DON'T THINK THAT'S IT. CHECK IT OUT...
SEE THAT GLOW? SOMETHING'S DEFINITELY AFFECTING THE CROWD...
HOW DO YOU LIKE JUMP CITY'S NEW LOOK, BRATS?
ISN'T IT FAB?
I KNEW MY SPELL AS D.D. AMMO WOULD SCRAMBLE YOU...
THAT VOICE... FAMILIAR...
"SPELL..." "SCRAMBLE..." WAIT A MINUTE, IF YOU REARRANGE THE LETTERS OF "D.D. AMMO," YOU GET...
MAD MOD!

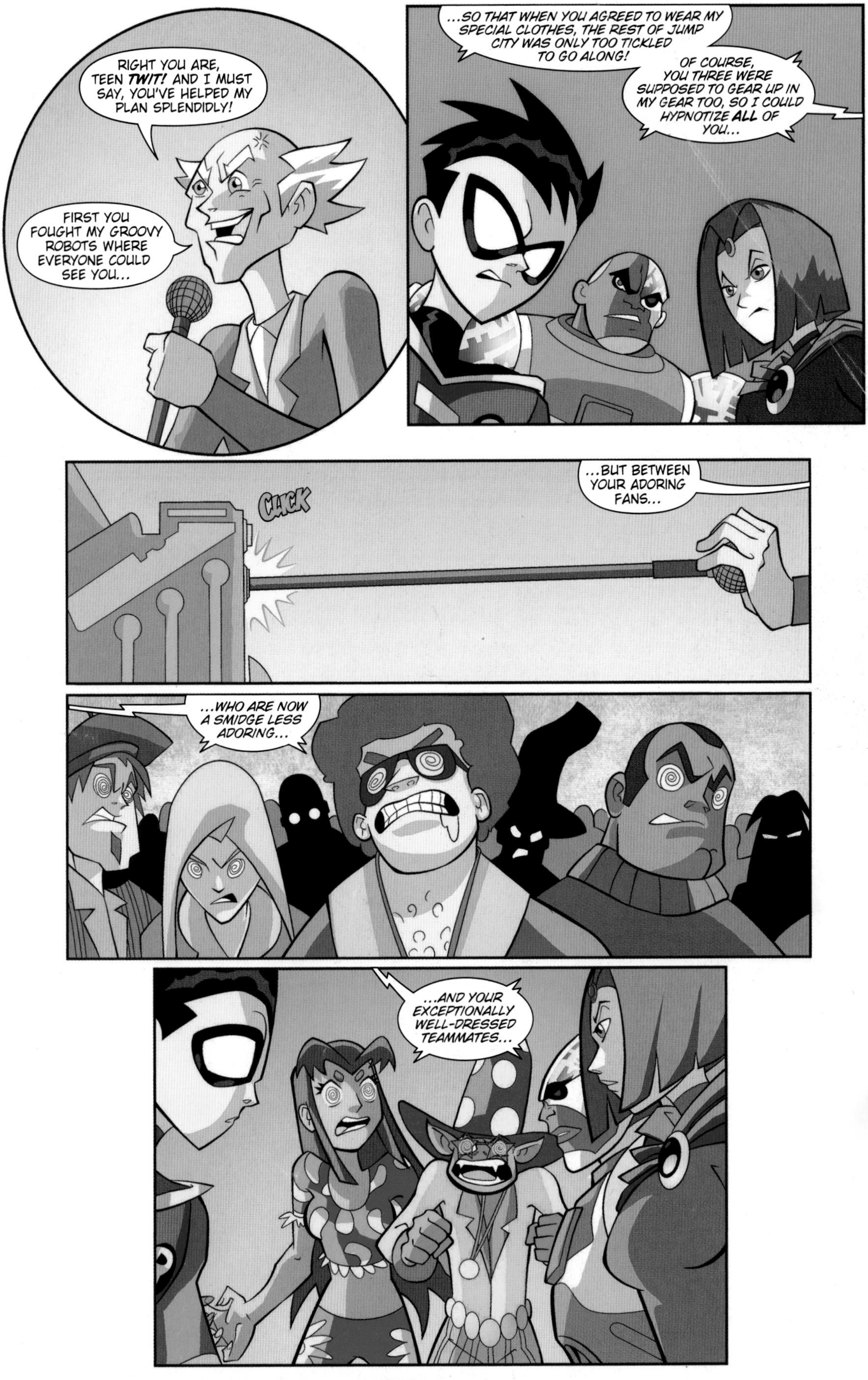
RIGHT YOU ARE, TEEN TWIT! AND I MUST SAY, YOU'VE HELPED MY PLAN SPLENDIDLY!
FIRST YOU FOUGHT MY GROOVY ROBOTS WHERE EVERYONE COULD SEE YOU...
...SO THAT WHEN YOU AGREED TO WEAR MY SPECIAL CLOTHES, THE REST OF JUMP CITY WAS ONLY TOO TICKLED TO GO ALONG!
OF COURSE, YOU THREE WERE SUPPOSED TO GEAR UP IN MY GEAR TOO, SO I COULD HYPNOTIZE ALL OF YOU...
CLICK
...BUT BETWEEN YOUR ADORING FANS...
...WHO ARE NOW A SMIDGE LESS ADORING...
...AND YOUR EXCEPTIONALLY WELL-DRESSED TEAMMATES...

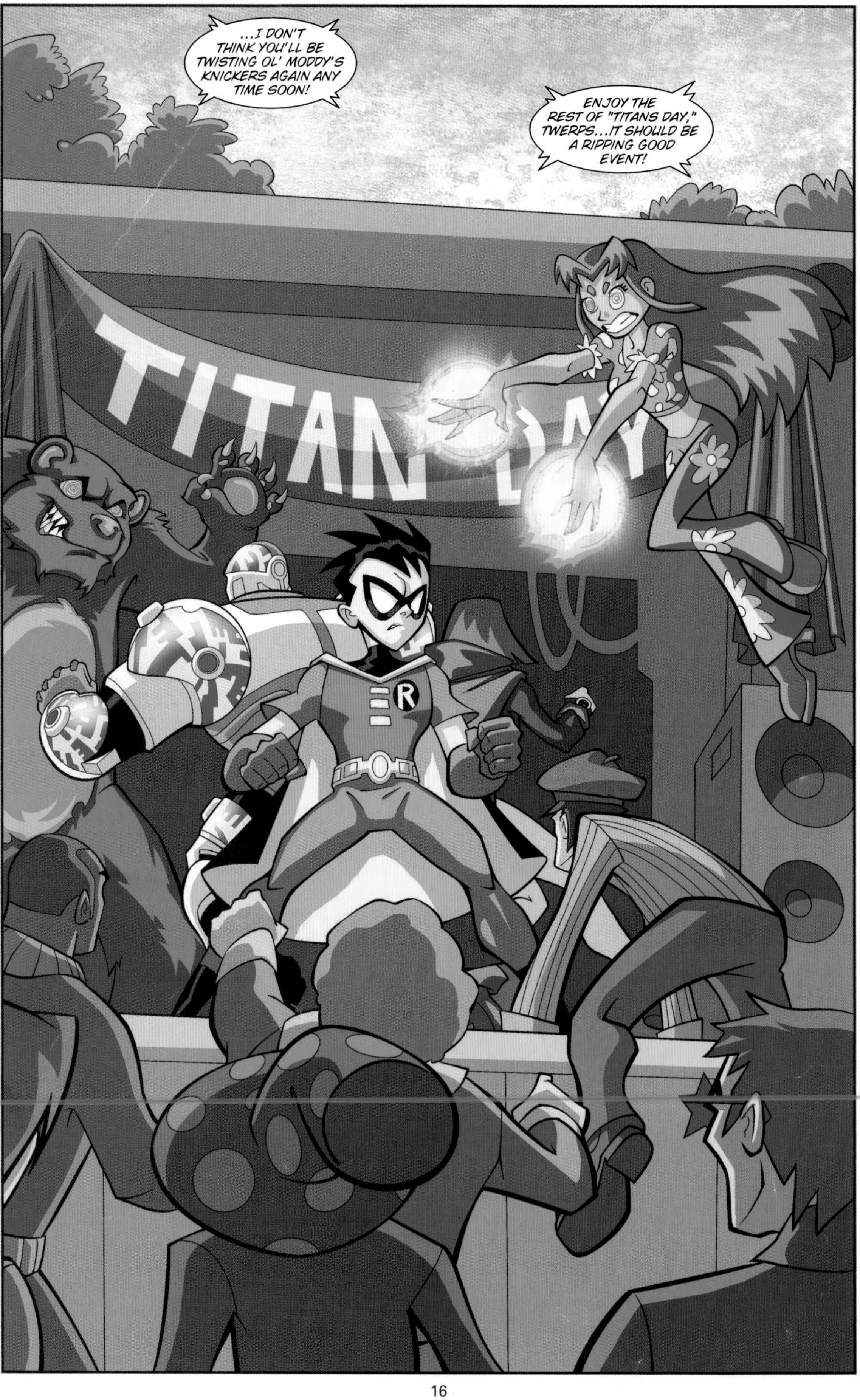
...I DON'T THINK YOU'LL BE TWISTING OL' MODDY'S KNICKERS AGAIN ANY TIME SOON!
ENJOY THE REST OF "TITANS DAY," TWERPS...IT SHOULD BE A RIPPING GOOD EVENT!
TITAN DAY

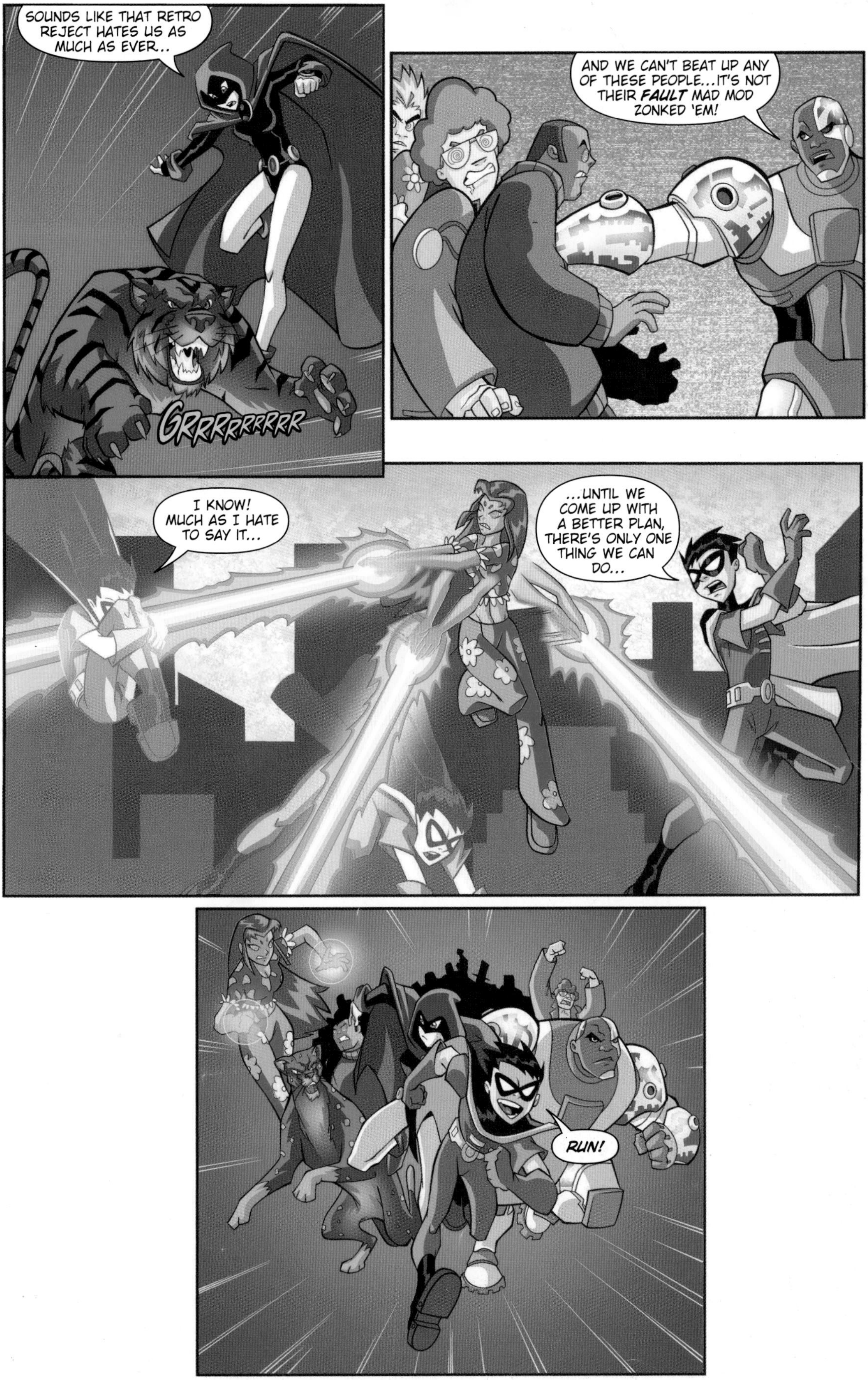

SOUNDS LIKE THAT RETRO REJECT HATES US AS MUCH AS EVER...
GRRRRRRRR
AND WE CAN'T BEAT UP ANY OF THESE PEOPLE...IT'S NOT THEIR FAULT MAD MOD ZONKED 'EM!
I KNOW! MUCH AS I HATE TO SAY IT...
...UNTIL WE COME UP WITH A BETTER PLAN, THERE'S ONLY ONE THING WE CAN DO...
RUN!

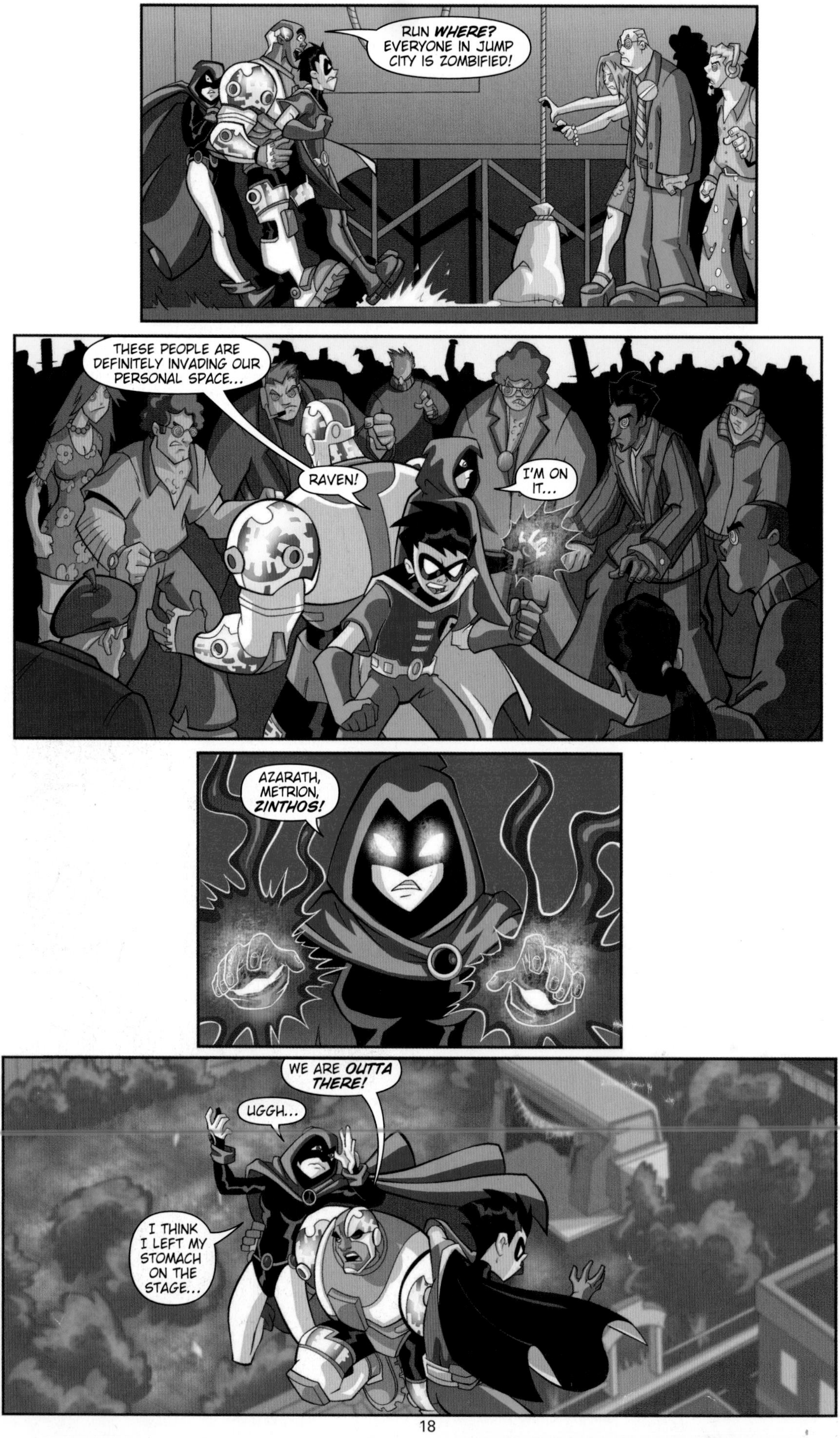
RUN WHERE? EVERYONE IN JUMP CITY IS ZOMBIFIED!
THESE PEOPLE ARE DEFINITELY INVADING OUR PERSONAL SPACE...
RAVEN!
I'M ON IT...
AZARATH, METRION, ZINTHOS!
WE ARE OUTTA THERE!
UGGH...
I THINK I LEFT MY STOMACH ON THE STAGE...

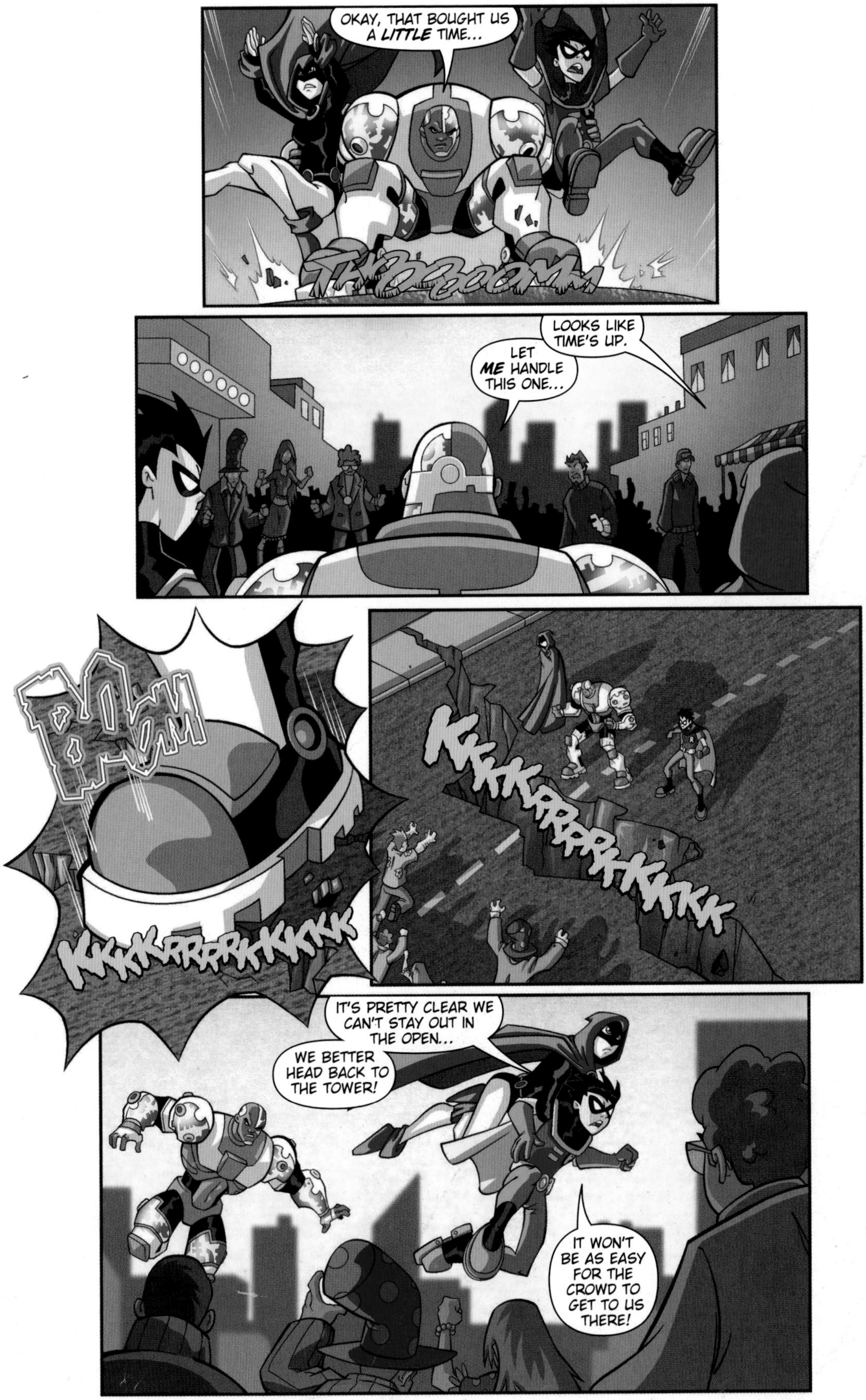
OKAY, THAT BOUGHT US A *LITTLE* TIME...
THOOOOOM
LOOKS LIKE TIME'S UP.
LET *ME* HANDLE THIS ONE...
BOOM
KKKKRRRRKKKKK
KKKKRRRRKKKKK
IT'S PRETTY CLEAR WE CAN'T STAY OUT IN THE OPEN...
WE BETTER HEAD BACK TO THE TOWER!
IT WON'T BE AS EASY FOR THE CROWD TO GET TO US THERE!

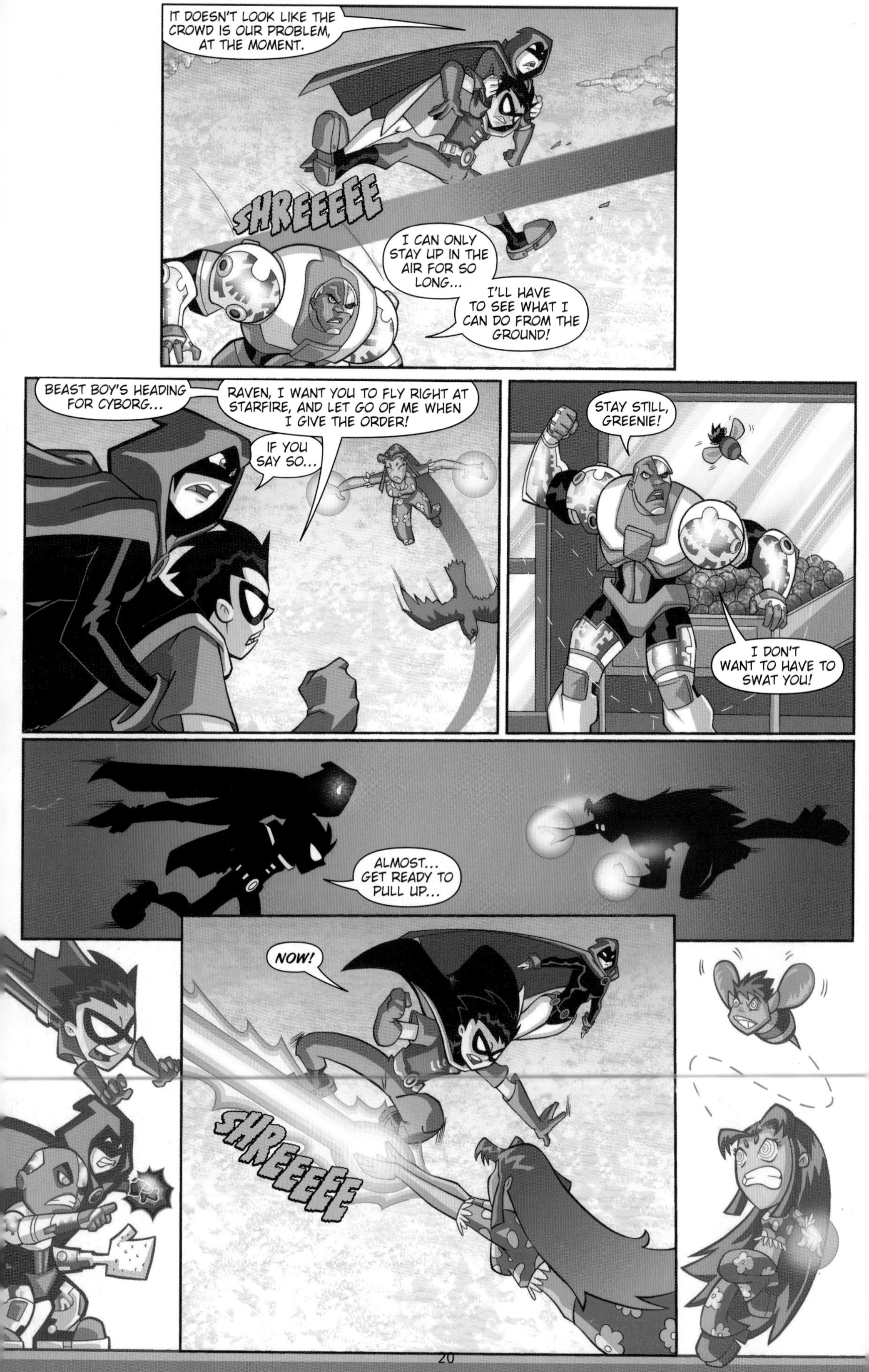
IT DOESN'T LOOK LIKE THE CROWD IS OUR PROBLEM, AT THE MOMENT.
SHREEEEE
I CAN ONLY STAY UP IN THE AIR FOR SO LONG...
I'LL HAVE TO SEE WHAT I CAN DO FROM THE GROUND!
BEAST BOY'S HEADING FOR CYBORG...
RAVEN, I WANT YOU TO FLY RIGHT AT STARFIRE, AND LET GO OF ME WHEN I GIVE THE ORDER!
IF YOU SAY SO...
STAY STILL, GREENIE!
I DON'T WANT TO HAVE TO SWAT YOU!
ALMOST... GET READY TO PULL UP...
NOW!
SHREEEEEE

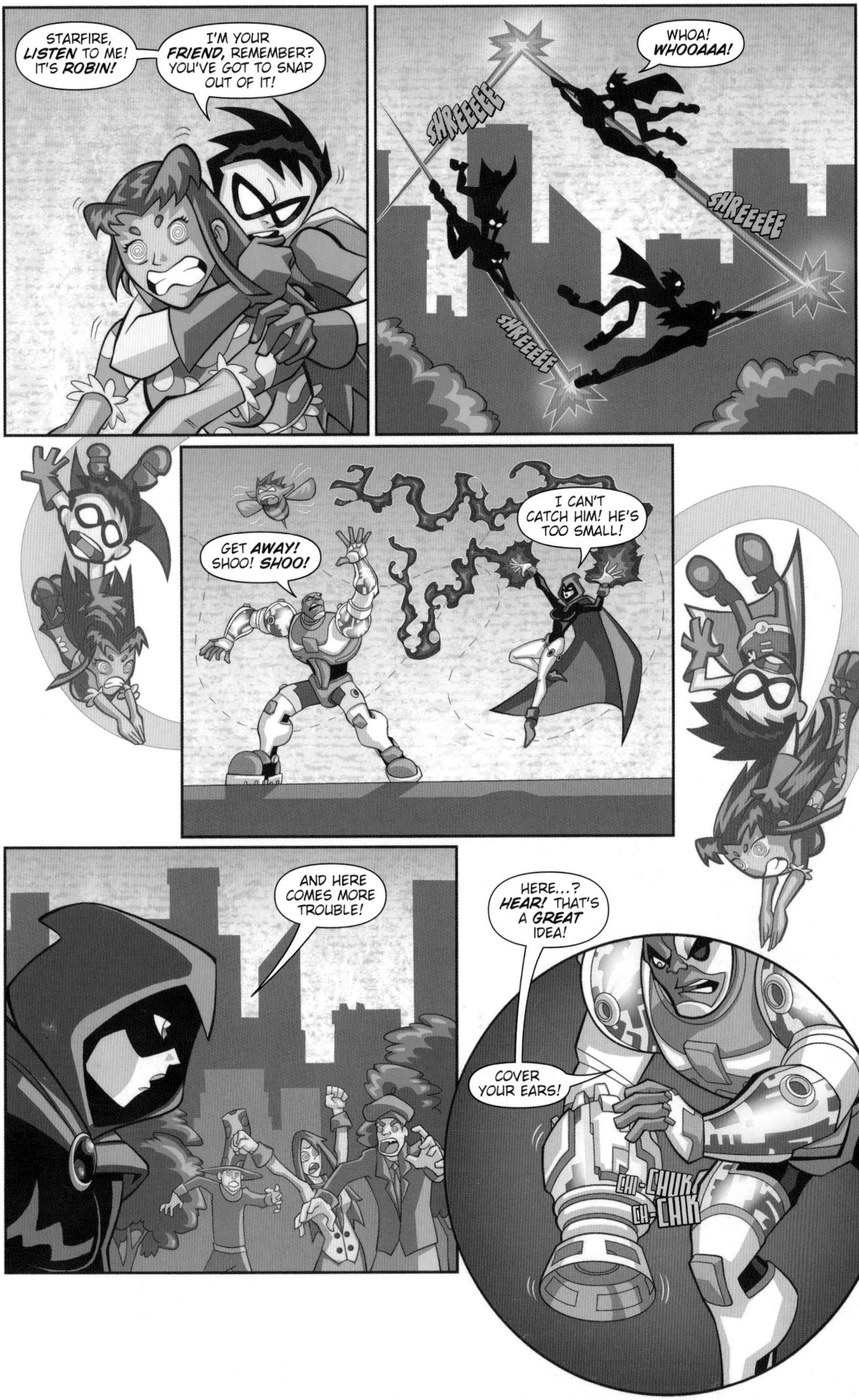
STARFIRE, LISTEN TO ME! IT'S ROBIN!
I'M YOUR FRIEND, REMEMBER? YOU'VE GOT TO SNAP OUT OF IT!
WHOA! WHOOAAA!
SHREEEEE
SHREEEEE
SHREEEEE
GET AWAY! SHOO! SHOO!
I CAN'T CATCH HIM! HE'S TOO SMALL!
AND HERE COMES MORE TROUBLE!
HERE...? HEAR! THAT'S A GREAT IDEA!
COVER YOUR EARS!
CHI-CHIK
CH-CHIK

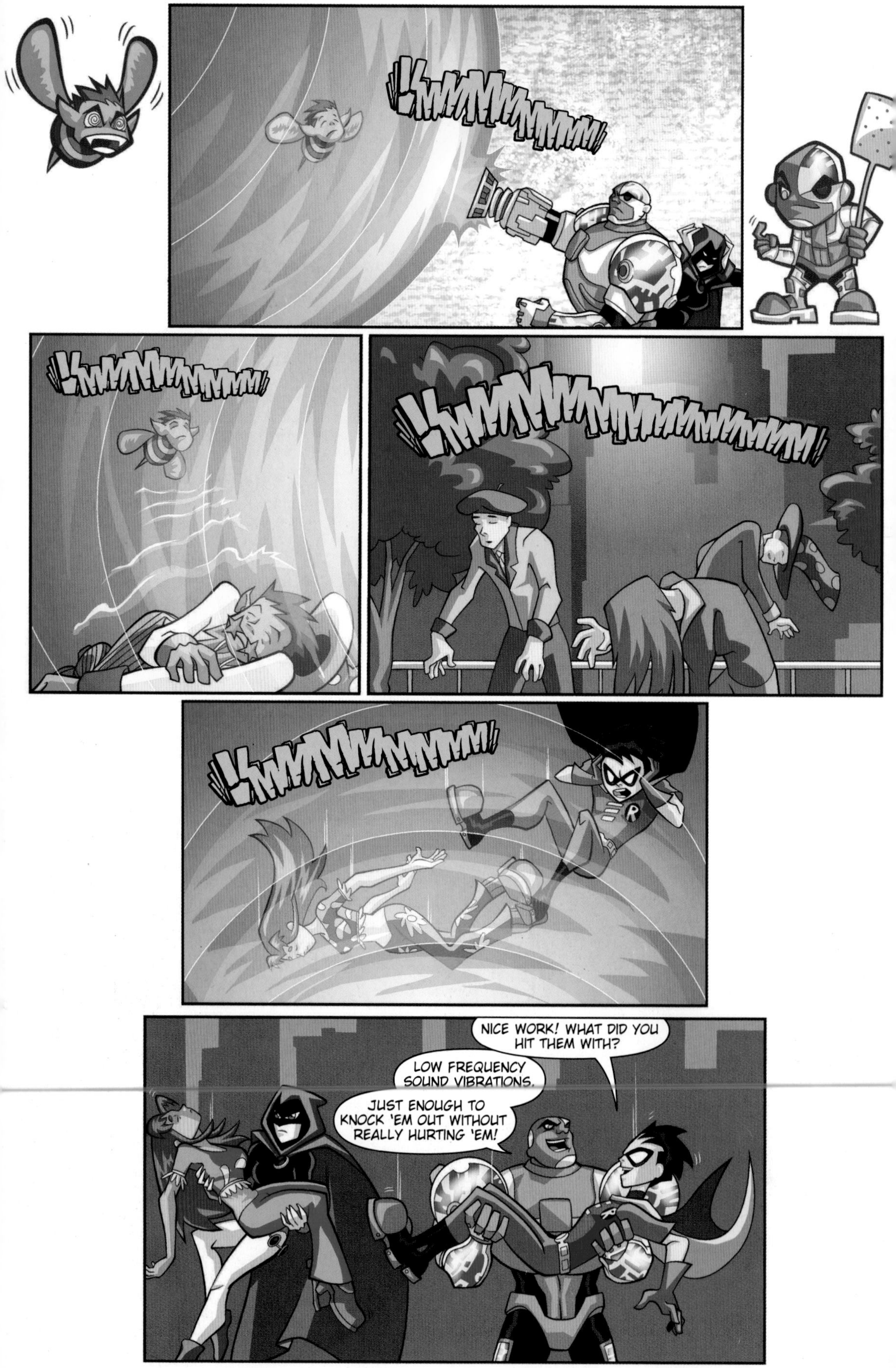
!SWMMMMMMMMMMM!
!SWMMMMMMMMMMM!
!SWMMMMMMMMMMMMMMMMMM!
!SWMMMMMMMMMMM!
NICE WORK! WHAT DID YOU HIT THEM WITH?
LOW FREQUENCY SOUND VIBRATIONS.
JUST ENOUGH TO KNOCK 'EM OUT WITHOUT REALLY HURTING 'EM!

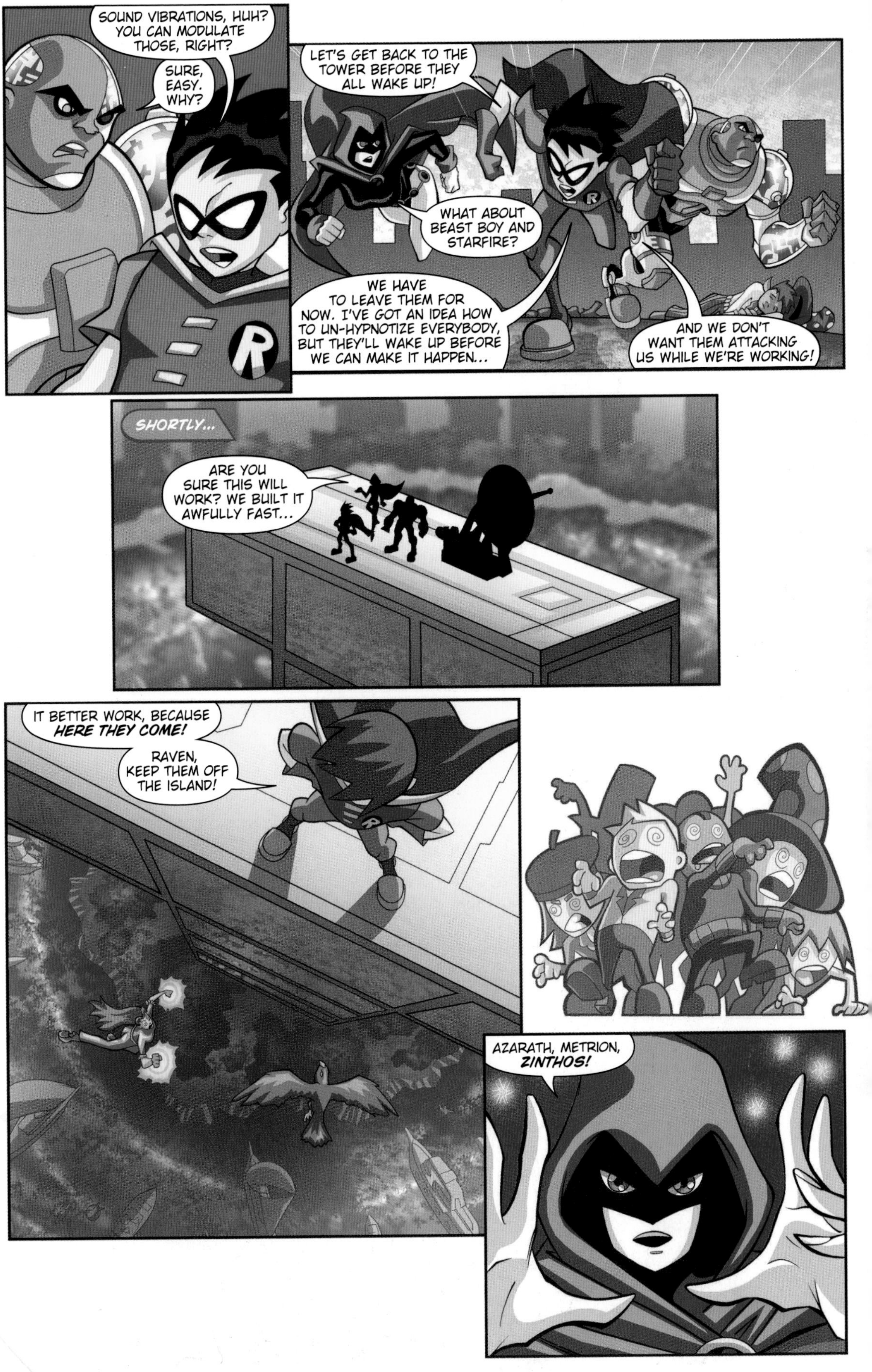

SOUND VIBRATIONS, HUH? YOU CAN MODULATE THOSE, RIGHT?
SURE, EASY. WHY?
LET'S GET BACK TO THE TOWER BEFORE THEY ALL WAKE UP!
WHAT ABOUT BEAST BOY AND STARFIRE?
WE HAVE TO LEAVE THEM FOR NOW. I'VE GOT AN IDEA HOW TO UN-HYPNOTIZE EVERYBODY, BUT THEY'LL WAKE UP BEFORE WE CAN MAKE IT HAPPEN...
AND WE DON'T WANT THEM ATTACKING US WHILE WE'RE WORKING!
SHORTLY...
ARE YOU SURE THIS WILL WORK? WE BUILT IT AWFULLY FAST...
IT BETTER WORK, BECAUSE HERE THEY COME!
RAVEN, KEEP THEM OFF THE ISLAND!
AZARATH, METRION, ZINTHOS!

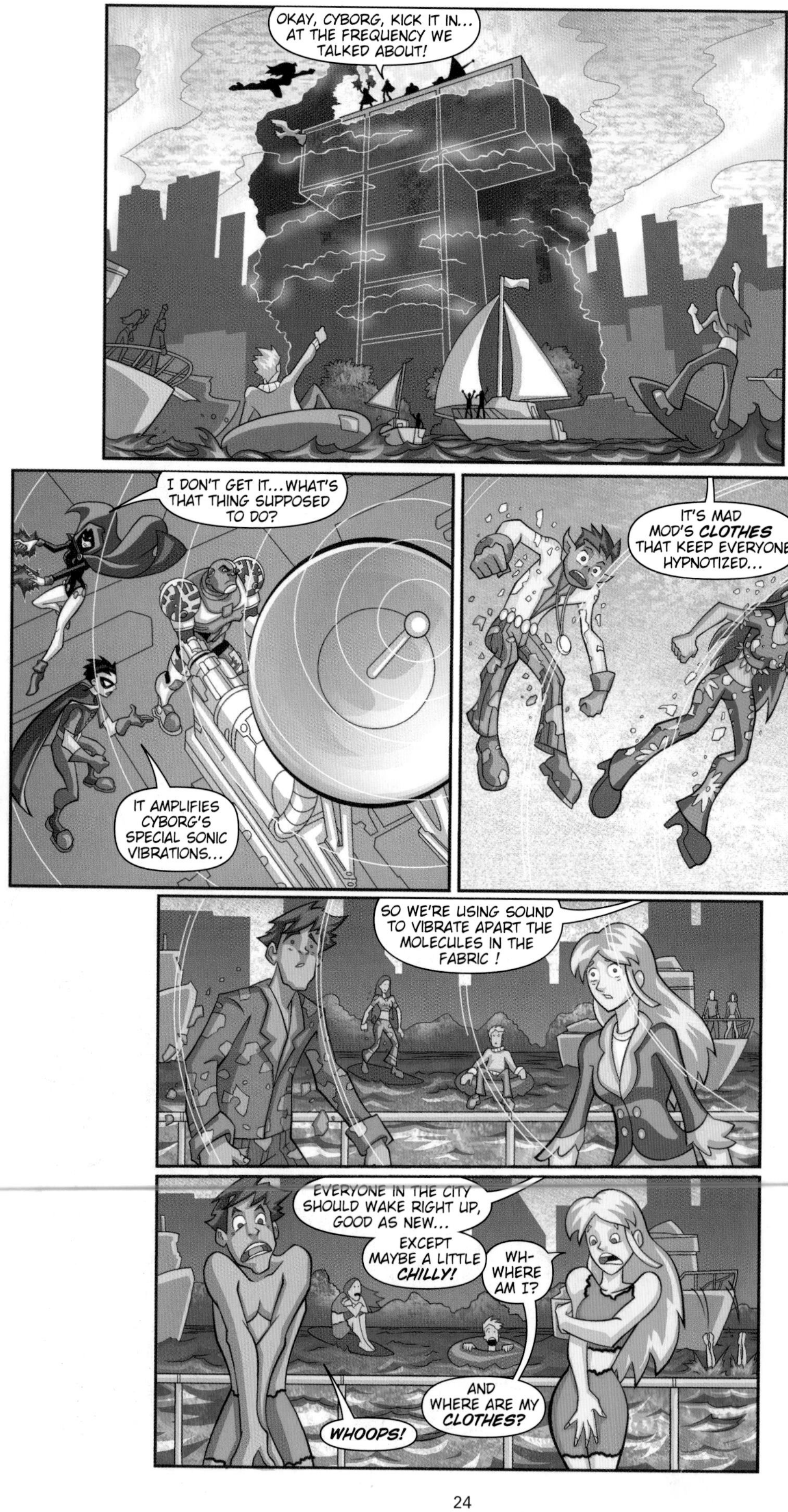
OKAY, CYBORG, KICK IT IN... AT THE FREQUENCY WE TALKED ABOUT!
I DON'T GET IT... WHAT'S THAT THING SUPPOSED TO DO?
IT AMPLIFIES CYBORG'S SPECIAL SONIC VIBRATIONS...
IT'S MAD MOD'S **CLOTHES** THAT KEEP EVERYONE HYPNOTIZED...
SO WE'RE USING SOUND TO VIBRATE APART THE MOLECULES IN THE FABRIC !
EVERYONE IN THE CITY SHOULD WAKE RIGHT UP, GOOD AS NEW...
EXCEPT MAYBE A LITTLE **CHILLY!**
WH- WHERE AM I?
AND WHERE ARE MY **CLOTHES?**
WHOOPS!

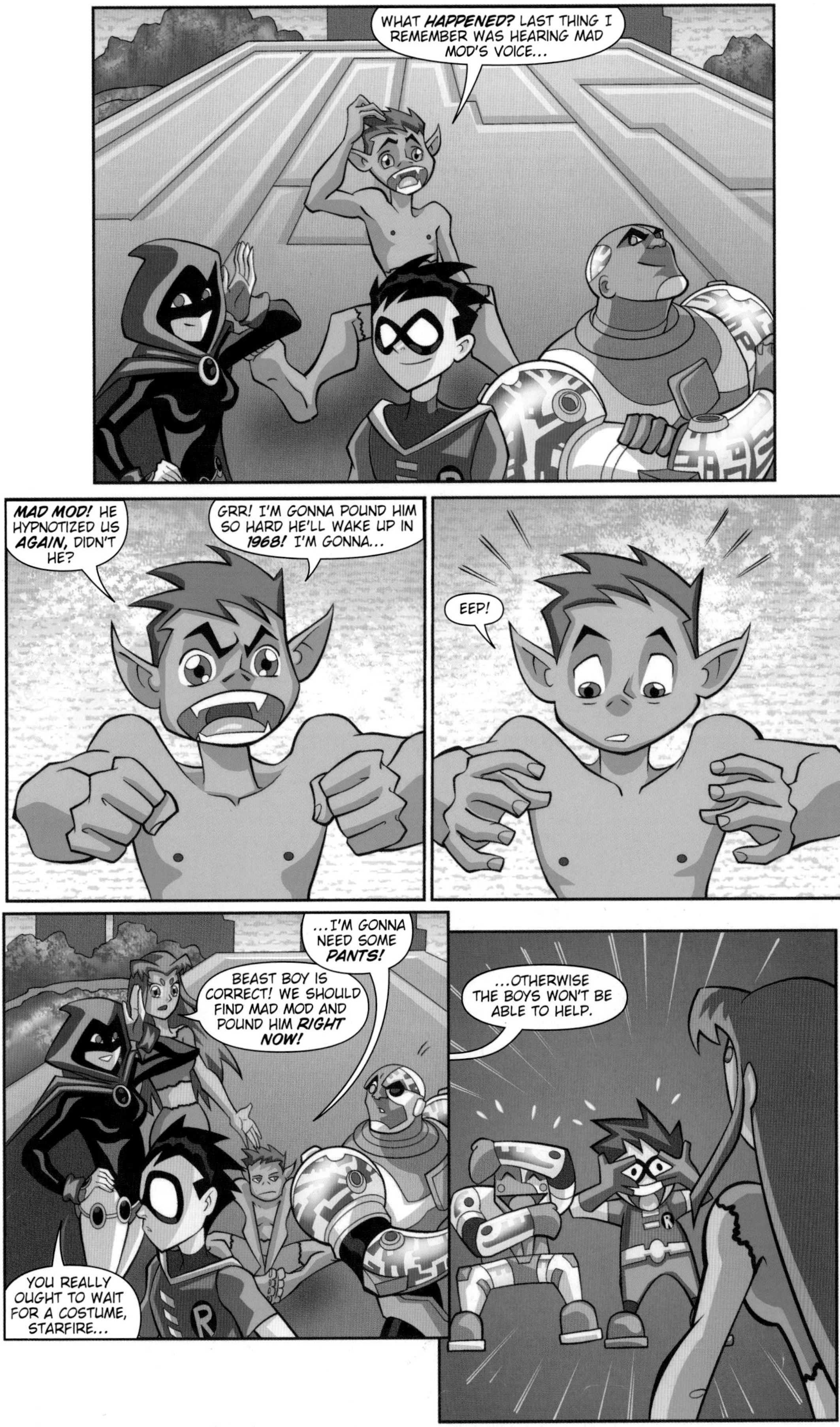
WHAT HAPPENED? LAST THING I REMEMBER WAS HEARING MAD MOD'S VOICE...
MAD MOD! HE HYPNOTIZED US AGAIN, DIDN'T HE?
GRR! I'M GONNA POUND HIM SO HARD HE'LL WAKE UP IN 1968! I'M GONNA...
EEP!
...I'M GONNA NEED SOME PANTS!
BEAST BOY IS CORRECT! WE SHOULD FIND MAD MOD AND POUND HIM RIGHT NOW!
YOU REALLY OUGHT TO WAIT FOR A COSTUME, STARFIRE...
...OTHERWISE THE BOYS WON'T BE ABLE TO HELP.

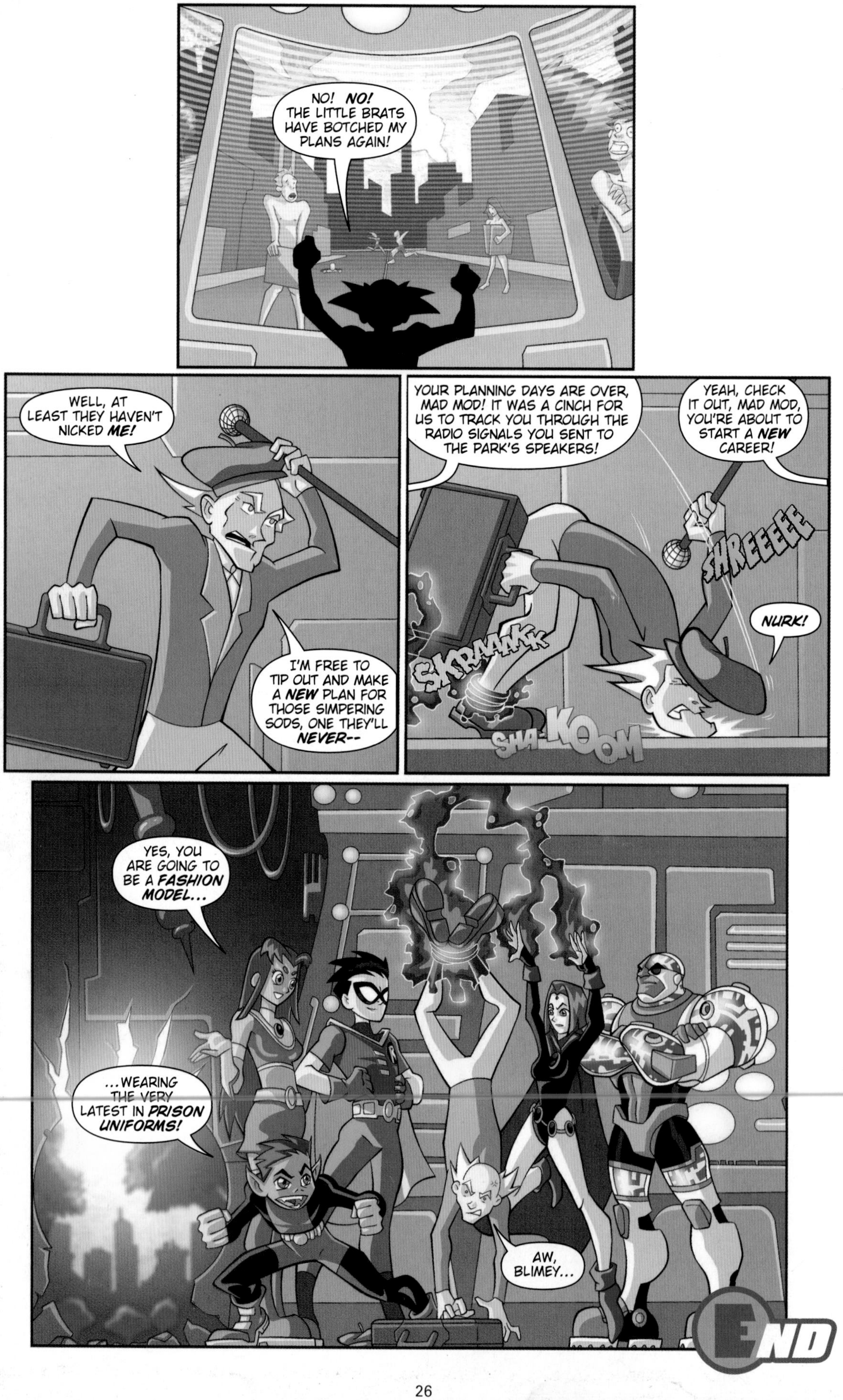
NO! NO! THE LITTLE BRATS HAVE BOTCHED MY PLANS AGAIN!
WELL, AT LEAST THEY HAVEN'T NICKED ME!
I'M FREE TO TIP OUT AND MAKE A NEW PLAN FOR THOSE SIMPERING SODS, ONE THEY'LL NEVER--
YOUR PLANNING DAYS ARE OVER, MAD MOD! IT WAS A CINCH FOR US TO TRACK YOU THROUGH THE RADIO SIGNALS YOU SENT TO THE PARK'S SPEAKERS!
YEAH, CHECK IT OUT, MAD MOD, YOU'RE ABOUT TO START A NEW CAREER!
SHREEEEE
NURK!
SKRAAAKKK
SHA-KOOM
YES, YOU ARE GOING TO BE A FASHION MODEL...
...WEARING THE VERY LATEST IN PRISON UNIFORMS!
AW, BLIMEY...
END

CREATORS

ADAM BEECHEN WRITER

Adam Beechen has written a variety of TV cartoons, including Teen Titans, Batman: The Brave and the Bold, The Batman (for which he received an Emmy nomination), as well as the live-action series Ned's Declassified School Survival Guide and The Famous Jett Jackson. He is also the author of Hench, a graphic novel, and has scripted many comic books. In addition, Adam has written dozens of children's books, as well as an original young adult novel, What I Did On My Hypergalactic Interstellar Summer Vacation.

ERIK VEDDER ARTIST

Eric began his career in art drawing pictures, which were very well received by his grade school friends. This eventually led to art school, where he learned how to sharpen pencils with his teeth. Finishing up his schooling, Eric then worked in the animation, video game, and comic book industries. He now practices the way of the samurai and works furiously on his never-ending story, Aardehn.

GLOSSARY

doom (DOOM)--very bad events or situations that cannot be avoided; death or ruin

exceptionally (ek-SEP-shuhn-ahl-ee)--especially, more than average, or unusually good

frequency (FREE-kwun-see)--the number of times that something (such as a sound wave or radio wave) is repeated in a set period of time

modulate (MOD-joo-late)--to change or adjust something

realized (REE-uh-lized)--understood something or achieved something

reject (REE-jekt)--a loser or someone who is undesirable

retro (RET-tro)--similar in appearance to styles or fashions from the past

scramble (SRKAM-buhl)--to move or act quickly to do, find, or get something

simpering (SIMP-er-ing)--smiling in a silly or fake manner

sonic (SON-ik)--of or relating to sound, sound waves, or the speed of sound

splendid (SPLEN-did)--very impressive

VISUAL QUESTIONS & PROMPTS

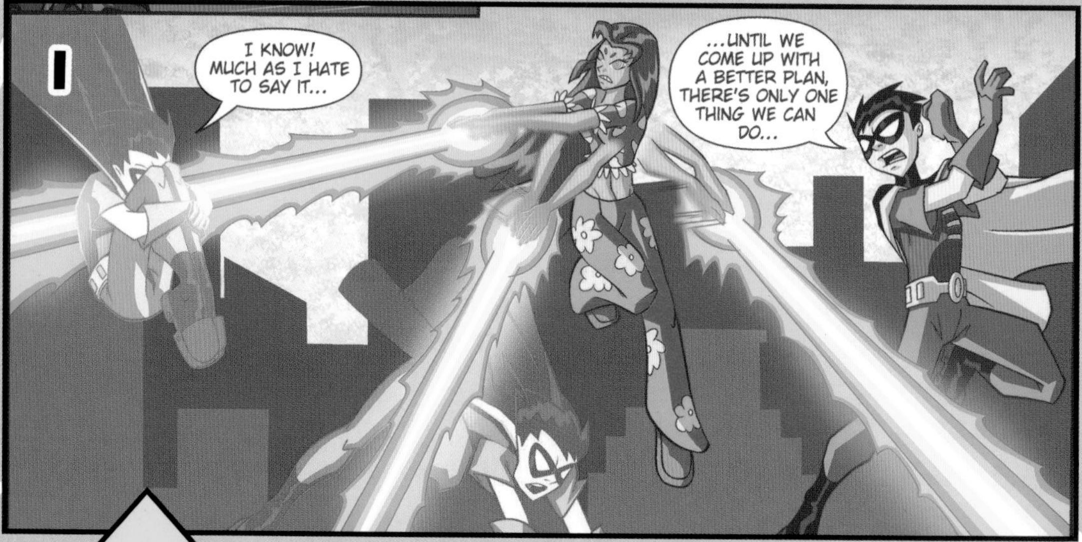
1
I KNOW! MUCH AS I HATE TO SAY IT...
...UNTIL WE COME UP WITH A BETTER PLAN, THERE'S ONLY ONE THING WE CAN DO...

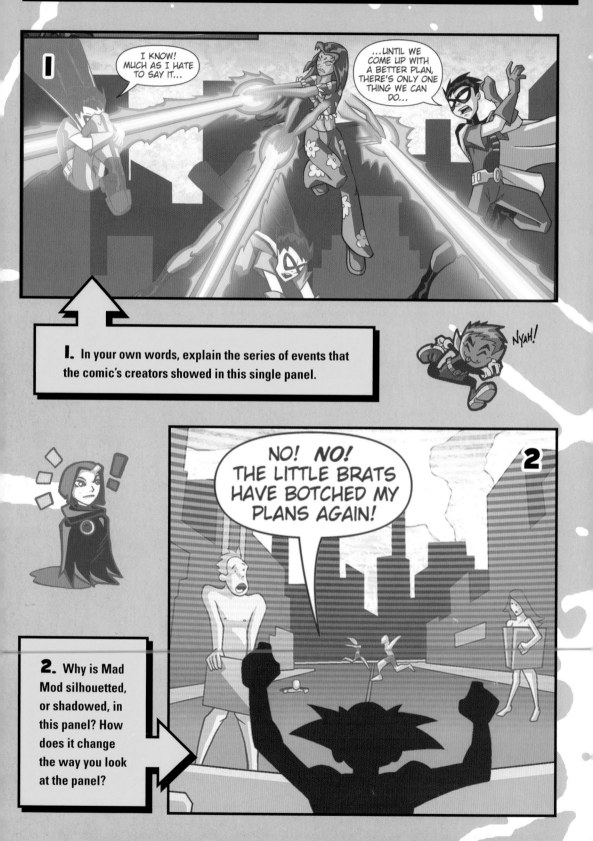

1. In your own words, explain the series of events that the comic's creators showed in this single panel.

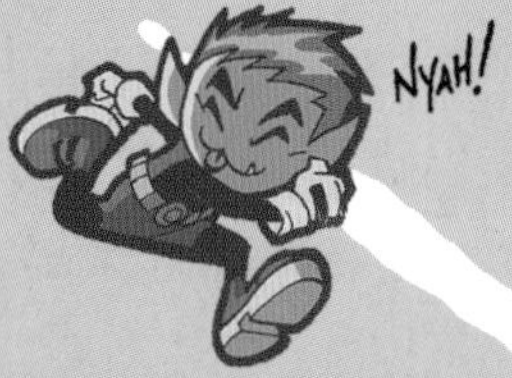
NYAH!

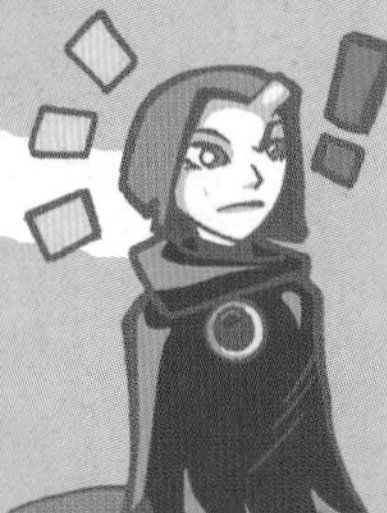

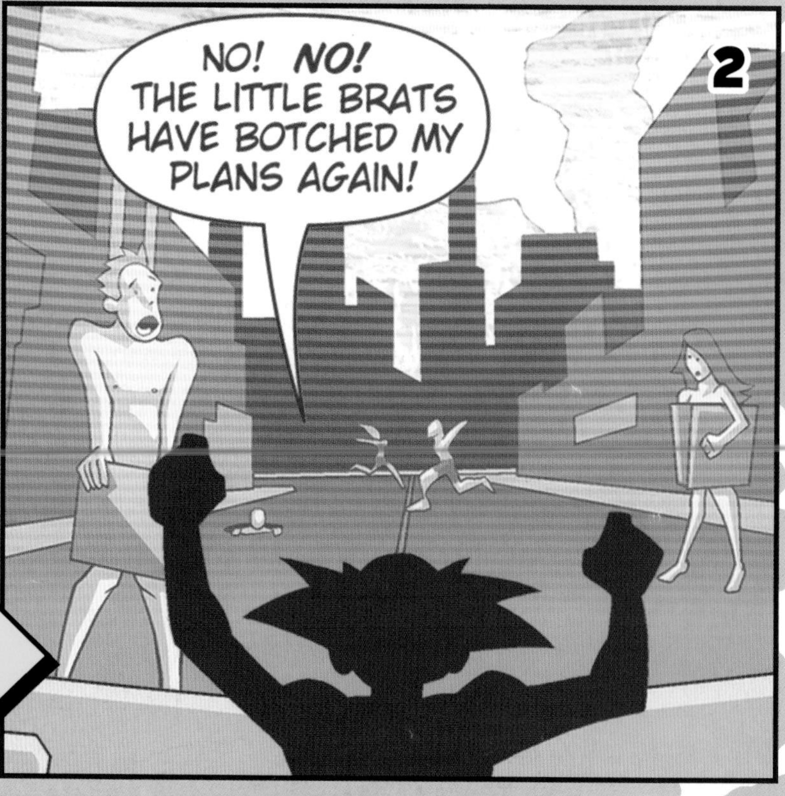
2
NO! *NO!* THE LITTLE BRATS HAVE BOTCHED MY PLANS AGAIN!

2. Why is Mad Mod silhouetted, or shadowed, in this panel? How does it change the way you look at the panel?

3. Beast Boy can shape-shift into any animal. Pick four animals and four situations where specific animals would be helpful.

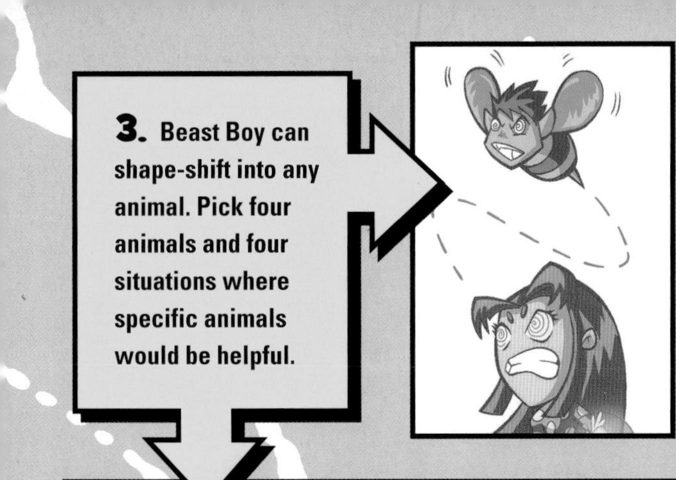

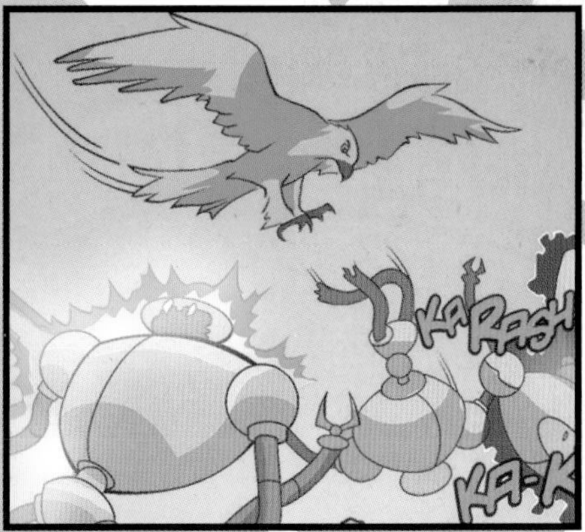
KA-RASH

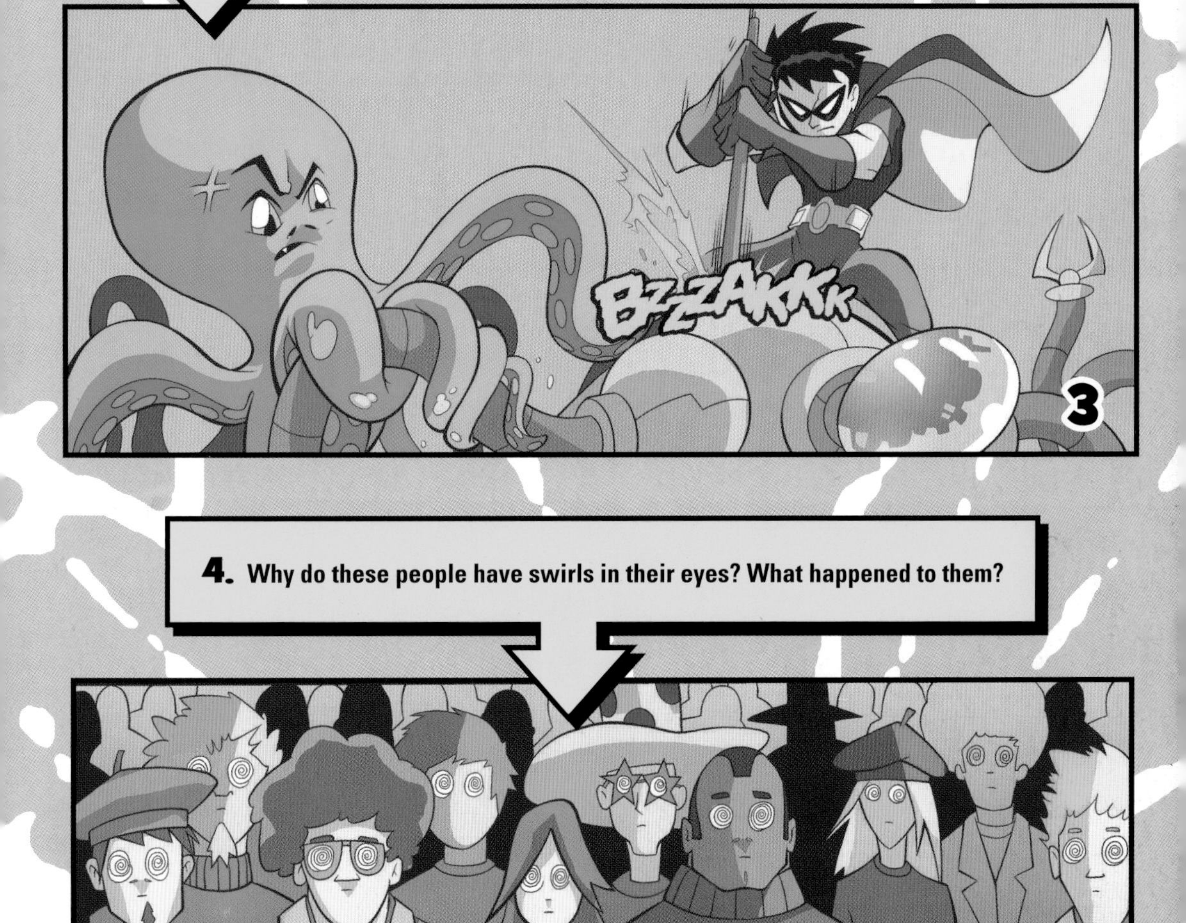
BZZZAKKKK
3

4. Why do these people have swirls in their eyes? What happened to them?

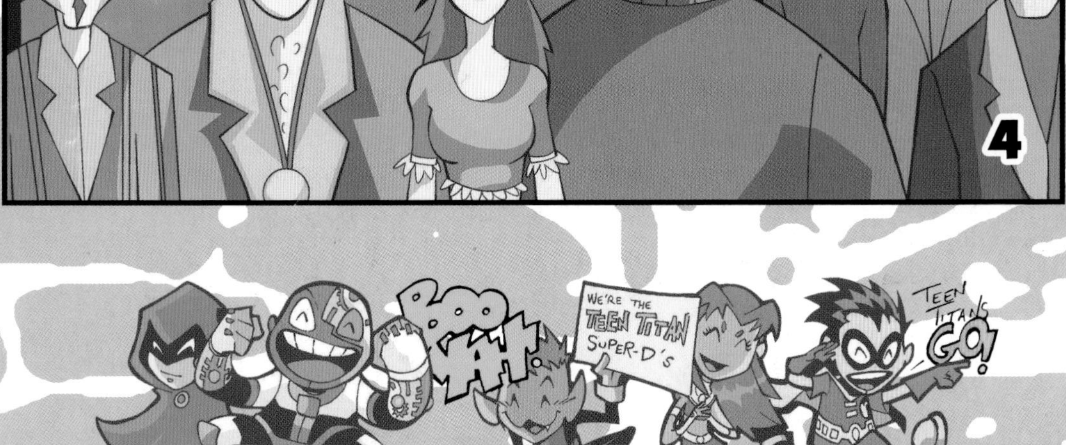
4

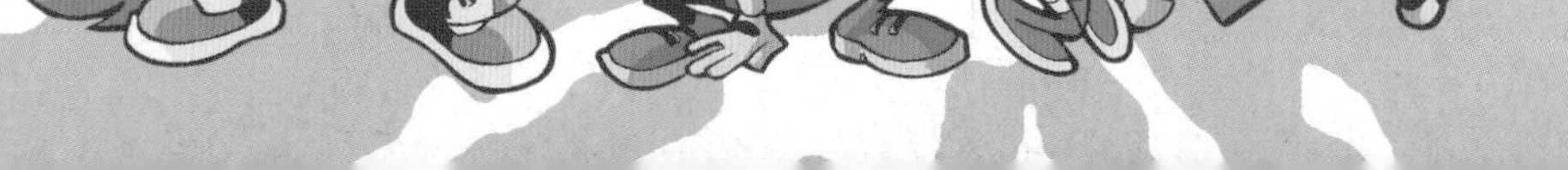
BOO YAH!
WE'RE THE TEEN TITAN SUPER-D'S
TEEN TITANS GO!

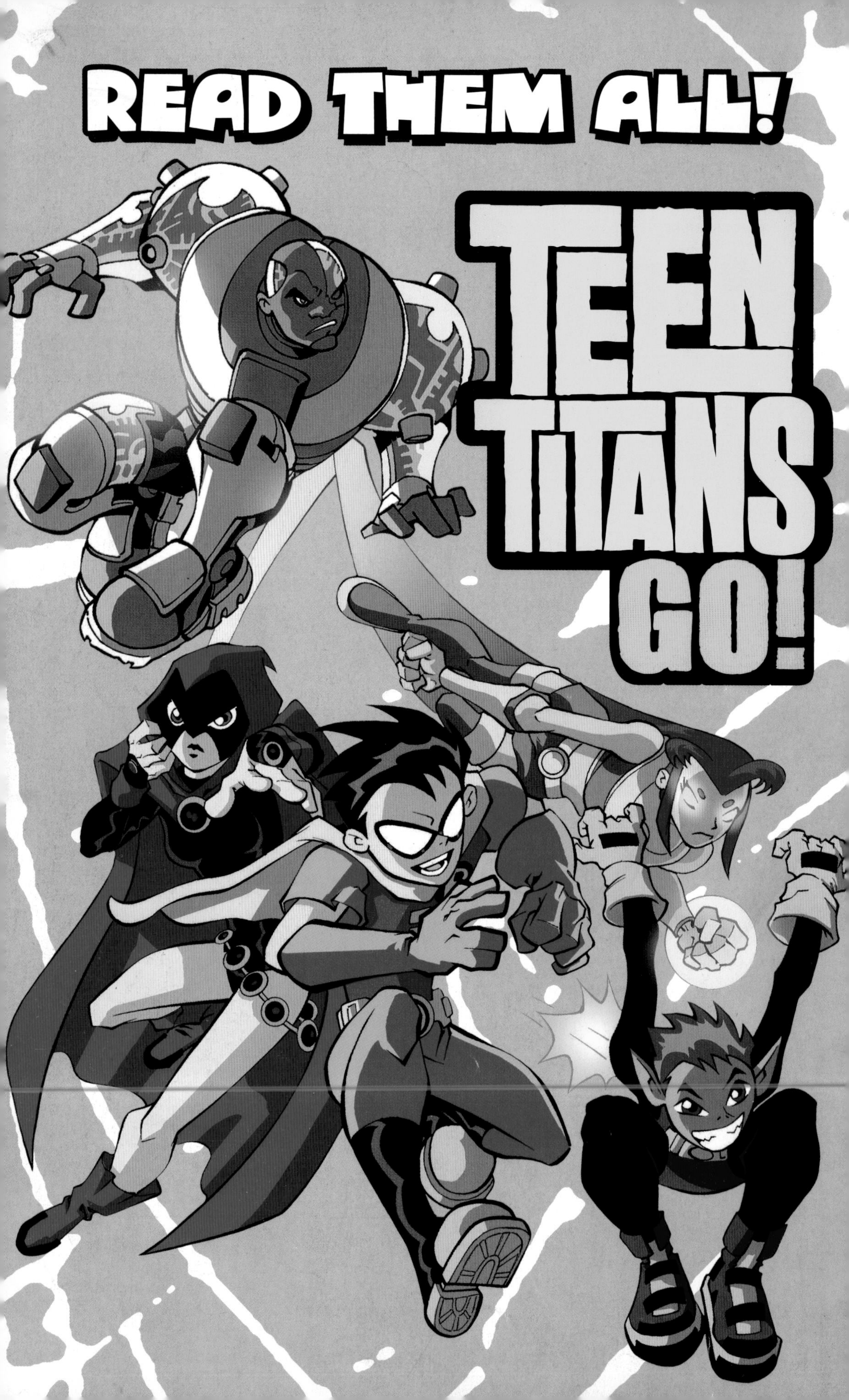
READ THEM ALL!
TEEN TITANS GO!